WILD HORSE
PUBLISHING

FRANKLIN HALL

Based on a true story

A Novel by Dave Southworth

Franklin Hall
By Southworth, Dave

Front and back cover design by Dave Southworth

Copyright 2010 by Wild Horse Publishing

ISBN: 978-1-890778-11-8
       1-890778-11-7

This novel is based on a true story. The names of most persons and some places are fictitious.

CONTENTS

WORKS BY DAVE SOUTHWORTH

BOOKS: NON-FICTION

Famous Gunfights of the American West
Feuds on the Western Frontier
Colorado Gold Dust: Short Stories and Profiles
Colorado Mining Camps
Ghost Towns and Mining Camps of the San Juans
Gunfighters of the Old West
Gunfighters of the Old West II
Famous Gunfights of Texas
Leadville

BOOKS: FICTION

Franklin Hall
Rhymes of a Storyteller

VIDEOS

Colorado Mining Camps: A Pictorial Treasure of the
      Gold and Silver Boom
Leadville: The Boom Years
Mining Camps of the San Juans
Cripple Creek and the Mining Camps of Teller County
The Mining Camps of Northwest Colorado
Boulder County Mining Camps: A Look Back
The Mining Camps of Gilpin and Clear Creek Counties
The Mining Camps of South Central Colorado

AUDIO BOOKS

Gunfighters of the Old West
Colorado Gold Dust: Short Stories and Profiles
Billy the Kid and the Lincoln County War
Jesse James and the James-Younger Gang
Doc Holliday and the Earp Brothers

FRANKLIN HALL

CHAPTER ONE

Setting the Stage

It was two weeks before we started back to school for our fall semester, and I was getting bored. I decided that it was time to liven things up a bit. The congregation at St. Theresa Catholic Church is full of old stuffed-shirts that need a little more humor in their lives. It is the perfect place and the perfect audience for a little of my foolishness.

Linda is my girlfriend. She is a pretty blond, but a little straight-laced. Linda always attends the late morning service at St. Theresa's each Sunday. Usually, she goes with her parents. Occasionally, I will escort her, when she is able to talk me into it. I am not very religious, but she was able to talk me into taking her to mass this particular Sunday.

Behind, and above, the altar, there is a large bank of organ pipes. Hidden from view is a platform at about mid-height in back of the pipes. I knew that the church would be totally empty between the early-morning and mid-morning services. So, I took the seven very loud wind-up alarm clocks that I had purchased the day before, climbed up on the platform, and hung them with wire coat hangers behind the organ pipes while the church was empty. They were set to ring at various times during the late-morning service. I left the church, and then drove over to pick up Linda. We stopped at a restaurant for breakfast, before heading to the church. As usual, the congregation was all dressed up. The ladies were in their fancy hats, and the men in their stiff collars. The priest was mumbling something in Latin when the first alarm sounded off. Holy shit, I thought, it echoed so well amongst those organ pipes. I couldn't help but snicker, and others snickered. The second alarm went off and the snickers turned to chuckles and laughs. As the others rang, the laughs turned to howls.

Linda looked at me, with a serious look on her face, and said, "You didn't have anything to do with that, did you?"

She knew me well. I said, "How could I have? I was with

you this morning."

I was 17 years old in September of 1955, as I entered my senior year at Kane Military Academy, a private military high school located on the east bank of the St. Johns River, south of Jacksonville, Florida. KMA was founded shortly after World War II, and is predominately staffed by former United States military personnel. The main building, Franklin Hall, was once a huge old three-story hotel. The ivy covered structure is constructed of coquina, a soft whitish limestone formed of broken shells and coral cemented together, and has several single level wood frame additions. One of those contains a large mess hall. The administrative offices, classrooms, library, commissary, main lounge, smoking lounge, and laundry are also located on the lower level. Two-thirds of the student body and several faculty members board in the dormitories on the second and third floors. My roommate and I are fortunate to have a third floor dorm room directly below the imposing tower that extends above the main entrance to Franklin Hall. We have no view of the river, but can see much of the 60-acre campus.

When the old hotel was converted into the school in 1948, a gymnasium and a swimming center were constructed on campus, as was a baseball diamond and football field with a long, narrow building that houses a concession stand with an announcer's booth above. Near Franklin Hall is a small coquina building that has a large iron door and bars over its two windows. It is the armory, and contains hundreds of M-1 rifles that the cadets drill and train with.

The four lane road that connects the highway with Franklin Hall turns into a circular drive in front of the main entrance. The circle that it encompasses contains a flagpole and cannon and is named the Major Jack Harden Circle, after the school's headmaster. Major Harden is a strict disciplinarian who believes that to spare the rod would spoil the child. So, the student body has another name for him and the circle, Major Hard-ass, and Hard-ass Circle. Our dorm room overlooks Hard-ass Circle.

Kane Military is an expensive school, so the cadets that board there are from affluent families, like mine. Dad owns controlling interest in a shipyard in Jacksonville. I work there every summer, reconditioning ships. At the end of each work day it always took about 15 minutes and plenty of mineral spirits to rid my body of industrial marine gray. The 1955-56 school year is my second at Kane. I have been promoted to the rank of corporal, and they made me a squad leader. Maybe they thought that a little extra responsibility would help keep me out of trouble, something that I had been in on a regular basis my first year. In fact, that is probably the reason Dad had me boarding at Kane, to keep me out of the house as much as possible, and to teach me some discipline. I was able to go home on weekends and holidays if I didn't have "Bull Ring," which meant work detail, and confinement, for getting into trouble. I had "Bull Ring" a lot last year. Most of the boarding students are at Kane for one of two reasons. Either they need discipline, or their father has a military background and wants them to have the same. There are a few parents that obviously don't know better, and send their kids to Kane anyway.

Kane Military Academy, an all-boys school, was named for Brigadier General Preston R. Kane, the school's founder. He purchased a defunct hotel, and land, and built the gymnasium and swimming center. Kane had a massive heart attack and passed away during my first year at KMA. When Kane died, Major General Eugene Franklin, became the Chairman of the school's Board of Directors. Franklin was the man who put up the money to refurbish the main building prior to the school's opening. It was for him that Franklin Hall was named. Major Harden was an educator who had served under Franklin during World War II. Franklin had recommended Harden to Kane for the position of headmaster.

Mrs. Bess Harden is one of only two women on the faculty. We, of course, call her Mrs. Hard-ass, because she is as dictatorial as her husband. The other female on the faculty, Miss Mary Ann Tolliver, is a cause for much heartache on campus because she is drop-dead beautiful, with a body that couldn't be any finer. We call her Miss Mary Ann, the only faculty member we are allowed to address by a first name. Miss Mary Ann teaches English 3 and English 4 (junior and senior English), which are possibly the only courses that students look forward to taking, besides physical education. Naturally, we have nicknames for all of the faculty members. Miss Mary Ann has several. There is Miss Bod, The Body, Miss Boobs, Miss Mary Can, and Miss Wet Dream, plus a few others that should go unmentioned.

I guess I should comment on Fulton Dames, a member of the faculty who lived on the third floor of Franklin Hall. He wasn't at Kane Military very long. Dames was appropriately named because he chased after women, especially Miss Mary Ann, who continually brushed him off. We nicknamed him Stud. In late October, Fulton Dames was permanently dismissed from the Kane staff after a night guard caught a young high school girl tiptoeing out of his room, with shoes in hand, at four a.m. one morning. Dames claimed that he was tutoring her. The school brass didn't buy the story, so he got the boot. She was young enough that he could actually have been teaching her a thing or two. I mention this incident because his replacement, Captain Bohanon, lived off campus and Dames' old quarters remained vacant for the rest of the school year. Somehow one of the cadets, Corporal Joe Crawford, obtained a key to the empty quarters. Crawfish, as we call him, wouldn't tell how he got that key, but it was great because we could sneak in there during free time and play poker, very quietly. All of the faculty quarters have keyed locks, while there are no locks or even door knobs on cadets' rooms. There is just a hole where the door knob used to be. Fulton Dames had been a chemistry teacher. When Bohanon assumed his duties we immediately nicknamed him BoBo.

Kane Military Academy is a four-year, secondary school, with grades 9 through 12. New boarding students receive a great deal of hazing, especially the freshmen and sophomores. Incoming juniors and seniors are hazed, but not nearly as much. The ridicule, criticism, and requirement to serve anyone with higher rank are worse than the initiation that a fraternity pledge goes through in college. The hazing is heavily frowned upon by KMA's administrative staff, but it goes on anyway, and usually lasts for a full school year. I had gone through some a year earlier, before joining the ranks of the hazers.

Boarding students generally look upon day students as a necessity to the financial success of KMA, but don't pay them much attention otherwise. They aren't part of the resident clique, so to speak. As a result, new day students don't get much hazing. They are also immune to Bull Ring. Normally, the worst punishment that a day cadet might receive would be extra time on the drill field, marching back and forth. It is called doing "tours." Day students were often helpful to the ones that boarded because they could "smuggle" necessities onto the campus any day of the week. Necessities like liquor and beer. We could always get things like cigarettes and toothpaste at the commissary.

Southside High School is located about three miles from Kane Military and is our biggest rival, in sports and otherwise. The otherwise part is what keeps some of us in constant hot water. Their kids have painted our highway sign with fruity colors, like pink. They sneak on campus and paint the cannon and bottom of the flagpole in Hard-ass Circle. One time they wrote a profane message in huge letters with powdered white lime, right in the middle of our football field. Well, needless to say, we retaliated. But, I'll get into all that a little later.

Whenever a boarding cadet is caught for doing something that the school brass disapproves of, he is usually confined to campus for one or more weekends and given "Bull Ring," which is a nasty work detail. Boarding students whose homes are in, or near, Jacksonville, like mine is, hate it the most. I especially disliked the confinement because I was going steady with Linda, who, although she lived in Jacksonville, was a boarding student at Hobart, a girls' school nearby, and it meant that I couldn't see her on those particular weekends. Linda didn't like it either when I had Bull Ring. My parents used to ground me when I did something wrong at home, but I could usually talk them out of it, so this was much worse.

Many boarding cadets have permission to keep their cars on campus, as I do, but they can't drive them off campus during the week, only on weekends. Hobart is another story, as is the panty raid on Hobart's dorm, but I'll also get into that a little later.

It seems as though Kane Military encourages smoking. The smoking lounge can only be used by those cadets who have written permission from their parents to smoke and use the lounge. It is off-limits to all other students. I have been smoking for a couple of years and have had my folks' consent to smoke and use the lounge. The smoking lounge is the best place to hang out on campus. There are two pool tables, two ping-pong tables, and several very comfortable lounge chairs. It almost takes on the air of a private club for smokers like me. Many trouble-making endeavors have been planned in the smoking lounge.

The armory is full of M-1 rifles, that will actually shoot, but there are no bullets. Blanks are used during dress parades by two members of the color guard, and by the crack drill team for certain salutes. Each cadet knows how to break down his M-1 and clean every part. Actually, I prefer doing that to drilling in the hot Florida sun.

Behind Franklin Hall, on the bank of the St. Johns River there is a boathouse that belongs to KMA. Inside is an old boat that was donated to the school by the Naval Air Station in Jacksonville. During my first year at Kane the boat was hardly ever used. It just sat there and gathered dust. I mention this because the boat would later become significant the day that Cadet Howard Hill goes berserk.

I am not sure that I ever knew his last name, but the mess hall was run by a large, colored man named Willie. He was easy enough to get along with, but sometimes stingy with the amount of food he cooked for the cadets, so there were times when he got picked on, and criticized.

There are three companies, two consisting of boarding students, and one that is made up of day students only. Day students commute daily, either by car or one of the two buses that Kane owns. So, there are three companies in the mess hall for lunch, but only two for breakfast and dinner. Each company consists of three platoons, and each platoon has four squads. Platoons will stagger their entrance into the mess hall, so as not to overwhelm the kitchen staff. When a platoon files in, each cadet takes his tin plate, tin mug, napkin, and eating utensils to his table. After each platoon is seated, two of its cadets go to the kitchen counter and bring back trays with whatever food is being served that day. Sometimes there is enough for seconds, if Willie had over prepared, but usually there wasn't. Many of the cadets had healthy appetites, and sometimes resented Willie because of the amount of food he served, or what the meal consisted of. I mention all this because evidently it triggered one of the first major incidents to occur on campus in September of 1955.

The dormitory rooms are large. There is usually one bathroom between two rooms, so normally four cadets share a bath. One big advantage to our tower room is that we have a private bath. A few other rooms do, as well. Every room has a closet. All of the cadet dorm rooms are furnished identically. Each has bunk beds, a double desk, two straight back uncomfortable desk chairs that face each other, two desk lamps, two dressers and one bookcase. Television sets (a relatively new invention), hot plates, and record players are not allowed. Each cadet can bring an alarm clock, a radio and a footlocker from home. During my first year I convinced the infirmary that I needed an easy chair for my back. They gave me written permission, so I brought in a very plush recliner that was the envy of all.

Oh, by the way, my name is Dean Bass. Most of the cadets call me Deano. A few call me Bass-ass.

CHAPTER TWO

Orientation

It is the day after Labor Day, 1955, the day of registration. The football team has been on campus for nearly three weeks, but everybody else is signing up, getting their room assignments if they are new boarding students, taking care of class schedules, books, uniforms, parking permits, smoking lounge passes, company and platoon assignments, and so forth. I had taken care of registration early this morning and picked up my books and new corporal stripes at the commissary. I am in the same room that I had last year, and my recliner hadn't been moved. As I pulled stuff out of my footlocker and began filling my dresser, a voice called out from the doorway, "Hey Deano, I'm your new roommate."

"That's great Squid, glad to have you. I thought they might assign a new guy. This is much better." Squid's real name is Marvin Brennan. His dad owns a fleet of charter fishing boats in Miami and he had his nickname long before he came to Kane Military. I said, "Take the top bunk, the right side of the desk, the empty dresser, and the left side of the closet," and then added, "How come you don't have the same room as last year?"

"Tommy's brother is here this year, so Tommy pulled strings and wanted his brother to room with him," said Squid. "I knew you didn't have a roomy, so I requested this room."

"That is so cool." I was delighted, because Squid is one of my best friends at Kane. "Hey, guess what."

"What?" he replied.

"They promoted me to corporal, and made me squad leader. Company A, 2nd Platoon, 3rd Squad."

"Are you shittin' me?" responded Squid, "They promoted me to corporal, Company A, 2nd Platoon and 2nd Squad leader. I'll be right in front of you in ranks."

"That's great," said I, "I can kick you in the ass any time I want to."

"Yeah, but once we do an about-face I'll kick you back."

"Yeah, I'm sure you would. Glad to have you as a roomy."

"Thanks," he said, "and man, I got a smoking permit this

year too."

"Glad to see that your dad came through. We can get in plenty of 9-ball."

"Or 8-ball."

"Yeah!" I said, with a big grin. Squid dragged his footlocker in from the hall, and began to unpack as we spoke. He removed a burgundy colored box with a gold cross affixed to the top and carefully placed it on top of his dresser. "What's in the little box?" I asked.

"Granny's ashes," responded Squid. "She died about two weeks ago."

"Granny's ashes? Are you telling me that your grandmother's remains are in that little box?"

"Yep!"

"That's spooky. Why are you carrying her remains around with you?" I asked.

"My grandfather is buried at Thorncrown Cemetery here in Jacksonville. Dad wants her to be close to him, so I have been instructed to make arrangements for a niche at Thorncrown for her ashes." As he spoke, Squid kissed two of his fingers and then placed them on top of the burgundy box.

Squid was a genius. He had a photographic memory, and made straight A's. I had made B- and C+ grades last year. It wasn't long before he taught me how to really study.

"Are you still going with Linda?" he asked.

"Still am. Although, sometimes I wonder why."

"Are you two having problems?"

"Oh no, it's just that she is so prissy. Sometimes I think that she has become a habit."

"Is she back at Hobart?"

"Oh yeah!" Hobart is a boarding school for girls from well-to-do families.

"Are we going to do that panty raid we talked about last year, but never did?"

"Yeah!" I said, "Linda and I have cooked up a plan, and it should work. Those girls over there are so horny, they will freak out."

"Think so?"

"Oh yeah, I know so."

"What classes are you signed up for?" he asked, and I told him. "Oh my God, we both have Miss Boobs fourth period, for senior English."

"Yep, and am I looking forward to that."

"Me too, I hope she wears a lot of tight shit like she did last year."

"She will."

"How do you know?"

"Her tastes aren't going to change in three months," I said.

"Damn," said Squid, "I'd like to roll around in a tub of body lotion with her, with both of us naked."

"You horny bastard. Did you ever get laid, or are you still a virgin?"

"Well," he said, "I came close, damned close."

"What the hell does that mean? Does it mean you felt a little tit? I can see we need to make a trip to the County Line and get you laid." The County Line is a truck stop with a row of trailers out back. It is a notorious whore house that none of us have ever been to, but we talk about it a lot. Supposedly, the truck stop is paying off the sheriff big time, to avoid being raided.

"Look, why don't you get Linda to fix me up with one of the chicks over at Hobart. Maybe one that's a little loose," said Squid, "You two get it on, so she probably knows other chicks that will."

"I can do that, but knowing you, it might take four months for you to get to first base. The best way to get you laid is to take you to the County Line."

"What do the girls look like over there?" asked Squid.

"What the hell does it matter," I retorted, "They are probably all fat with warts on their noses, but at least you'll get laid."

"Well, maybe." He hesitated, "But you've got connections, why don't you find out what the girls look like?"

"Look," I said, "You may get to choose a good looking one, and if not you can always refuse an ugly one."

"Maybe not," he said, "What if they make me pay in advance, then send me to a trailer with an ugly one?"

"The worst thing that could happen is that you get laid."

"How much does it cost?" said Squid.

"What the hell do you care? You have plenty of money. Stop making excuses. We are going to go over there."

Well, we didn't get over there right away, but we kept talking about it. It was inevitable though, we were destined to go sooner or later.

During the next two weeks we got settled into our classes and various routines. Each evening, after dinner, there was a mandatory study period from 1800 to 2000 hours. All cadets had to be at their desks, with their doors open so the officer on duty could check each room. It amazed me that Squid never studied, yet he always made A's on his quizzes. He would sit at his desk reading comic books, or girly magazines while he dreamed of the day he would get laid. He often became very engrossed in *Dick Tracy* comics, but rarely ever his school books. When I asked him how he did it, he explained.

"Look Deano, it's simple. Just about every question on every test that an instructor gives is from material that has been covered in class. If you stay focused and memorize everything that is covered, you will never need to open your textbooks."

"That may be easy for you, Squid, because you have a photographic memory, but I could never memorize everything that is covered in class."

"It is easier then you think. Try it. You may forget some things, but when they pop up again on a quiz, your recall will bring them back. Forget the textbooks. Start out by taking brief notes in class, and the key is the word brief. Then scan your brief notes during study period. They will bring back everything you need to remember. Eventually you will train yourself to remember all that is said in class, and you won't need any notes. After you have mastered that, we can sit here and play chess for two hours every evening."

"I don't know if I can do it," I said, "but I'll give it a go and see what happens."

It was the best advice on studying that anyone had ever given me. All of a sudden my grades jumped up and I was making A's. Before long I was a National Honor Society student, like Squid. But, unlike Squid, I didn't waste my time reading comic books during study period.

Each time that Squid was near his dresser, he would kiss two fingers and place them on top of the box holding Granny's ashes. "I wish you would take Granny's ashes over to Thorncrown. It is like sleeping with a ghost in the room with her remains sitting there," I said.

"Oh I will, once I have time to make the proper arrangements," responded Squid.

Miami was too far to go on a weekend so Squid would often check out from school with my address as his destination. We had three guest rooms at the house so he was more then welcome. Mom didn't have to go to any extra trouble because we had a full-time colored cook, Susan, and a white live-in maid, Tina. Susan left about 7 p.m. every evening, except when the folks were entertaining. Tina lived in the maid's quarters which consisted of a bedroom, bath and sitting room. We had an eight bedroom house on the Ortega River. Of course, Dad, Mom, my sister Carrie, and I each had our own rooms, as well. Yeah, Dad and Mom had separate rooms, but they didn't always sleep in their own bedroom. Once in a while Mom would wake up in Dad's room, so Carrie and I assumed they were still getting it on.

The first time this semester that Squid came home with me, we had to amuse ourselves. Linda had fixed Squid up with one of the girls from Hobart, and I was right he didn't get to first base, but we had fun anyway. We were in downtown Jacksonville. I was driving, and Squid was in the trunk with his arm dangling out so everybody could see it. His lower arm and hand were covered with ketchup. With his other hand he held the lid down as far as it would go. Right in front of a crowded bus stop, I slammed on the brakes, jumped out, shoved his arm inside and closed the trunk, while the horrified crowd watched in amazement. Once I had rounded a couple of corners, I stopped to let Squid out of the trunk. We cracked up, in fact, Squid and I laughed about that foolishness for several days. Linda wasn't too impressed.

"You could give somebody a heart attack doing things like that," she said.

Linda was great but she didn't have enough fun in life, I thought. She was sweet, but she was also prissy and pissy.

CHAPTER THREE

Willie's Coffin

Squid's 1954 Ford was newer and nicer then my 1946 brown Oldsmobile sedan, that everybody called the "turdmobile," because it looked like a big turd rolling down the highway. So, we usually took his car when we went places together. Boarding students had to check back in at school by 9 p.m. on Sunday evening, unless they had special leave allowing them to stay out until 30 minutes before first period on Monday morning. Well, we had special leave, but overslept a little on Monday. Squid was putting the pedal to the metal to get us back to Kane on time. All of a sudden, from out of nowhere, there was a red light flashing right behind us. We pulled over.

"Boy, don't you know the speed limit on this highway?" the cop asked Squid.

"Yes sir!" said Squid, "Its 55."

"I clocked you boys at 87 miles per hour. Let me see your driver's license." The cop took Squid's license and returned to his patrol car while we sat and waited. "Man, we are going to be A.W.O.L. in twenty minutes, and that probably means Bull Ring," said Squid.

"You're right about that," I said in agreement. In a few minutes the officer returned and handed Squid a ticket and his license.

"You have fifteen days in which to pay your fine or appeal if you wish to do so," stated the cop. "I see you boys are Kane students," he added. He could tell because we were wearing our uniforms. "I am going to follow you the rest of the way to your school, so don't speed."

After we had gone another mile, the cop turned off, and Squid floored his accelerator. I could tell he was really pissed off. "Don't sweat it man, I'll split the fine with you," I said.

"You should pay the whole shittin' thing," he said, "it was your mother's alarm clock that didn't go off."

"Okay, I'll pay the whole shittin' thing."

"I'm just joshin' you man. I was driving. I'll pay the fine."

We made it back to Kane in the nick of time, to avoid getting into trouble.

That night during study period, Squid asked me if I had plenty of staples. I told him that I had a whole box full, and passed them over to him. He took the speeding ticket and a twenty dollar bill, to cover the cost of the fine, and proceeded to staple them together. Well, he stapled and stapled putting hundreds of staples into that twenty and that ticket. Eventually, when he couldn't get another staple into that silver brick, he wrapped it in brown paper, addressed a label, and then set it aside to mail the next day. The whole time that he went through that process he was cussing the cop that wrote the ticket.

"Well, speak of the devil!" I said, "Look down at Hard-ass Circle, Squid. Two cop cars just pulled in."

"I wonder what's going on."

"I have no idea, but there goes Hard-ass out to talk with them."

Major Harden and the patrolmen walked around the end of the building toward the mess hall. Thirty minutes later the police climbed back into their cars and headed toward the highway.

"That was strange," said Squid.

"I'm sure there is some explanation. We'll probably find out what happened tomorrow morning."

All hell broke loose on Tuesday morning. It seems as though someone had gone to a lot of trouble to frighten Willie, the colored man who runs the mess hall. After hearing a knock Monday night on the door of his apartment adjacent to the mess hall, he opened the door and found a small cardboard coffin with a little colored doll in it. Stuck in the doll were several hat pins, with red blood carefully painted at the point of puncture of each pin. There was a note attached that read, "Get out of town nigger or the Ku Klux Klan will tar and feather your fat ass." Well, needless to say, Willie went straight to Major Harden with the coffin in hand. Hard-ass then called in the Battalion Commander, Joseph Absalom, who was the highest ranking cadet. The major also called the police.

When reveille sounded at 500 hours on Tuesday, all cadets were out in their respective halls, in their pajamas, at attention. It seems as though we stood there forever while a thorough inspection of every room took place. Inspections were usually conducted by the highest ranking cadet officers, but a few faculty members got involved in this one. All wastebaskets were turned upside down, and the contents were sifted through with great care. Dresser drawers and footlockers were opened, as were any boxes found in closets. Eventually, we were all allowed to return to our rooms, put the trash back in our baskets, make up our beds, shower, dress, and march to breakfast. All of us, that is, except for Private Elvin McCall who was taken to Harden's office for interrogation. Breakfast was two hours late, and our first two class periods were canceled. Willie was noticeably absent from the mess hall during breakfast that morning.

When fourth period rolled around, Miss Mary Ann seemed extremely concerned with what happened, as most women would be. By then we had a partial explanation. It seems that McCall's wastebasket had scraps of cardboard in it that matched those pieces that the coffin was made from. McCall's roommate was sick in the infirmary, and had been for over 24 hours, so he couldn't have been involved. Elvin McCall was a little beebee eyed guy that most of us thought was strange. In fact, Squid had said that McCall reminded him of B.B. Eyes, one of the gangsters in his *Dick Tracy* comic books.

Early that same afternoon, McCall was expelled from Kane Military Academy. He was not punished in any other way, by either the school staff or the police. It was not uncommon in 1955 for Negroes to be harassed by members of the white race. Although the school hires colored help, no colored students or females of any race are allowed to enroll at Kane. The school staff probably had no choice, however, but to expel McCall. It had to maintain certain principles, and didn't need a rotten apple in the basket.

Elvin McCall packed up his stuff, and tried to sell his uniforms and books, but had no takers. His father's chauffeur arrived that evening to pick him up in a limousine. That was a dirty thing McCall did to Willie, so we didn't even bother to tell the guy goodbye.

CHAPTER FOUR

The County Line

Most of us hated to drill. Lt. Bones Gifford was our platoon leader. He was aptly named for he was a skinny guy. He was a brown-noser who would always do anything his superiors desired. He also drilled his platoon very hard, much to our displeasure. On rare occasions, when he was absent, Sgt. Bradford Marin, second in command, would take over. That was great because Brad usually marched us straight into the woods for 30-minute cigarette breaks. Brad was one of my best friends and part of our little clique. Usually when we planned something crazy, he was in on it.

Well, here it was October, and Squid still hadn't been laid. I decided that we had talked about that matter way too long. It was time to go to the County Line truck stop. Linda's family was going out of town, so she planned to stay at Hobart for the upcoming weekend. She certainly didn't need to know what we were up to, so it was the perfect time to get Squid laid. I decided that Saturday would be the best day, and told Squid. As the weekend approached, Squid sure got nervous, real nervous.

"Should I wear a rubber?" he asked.

"Depends on whether you want to get syphilis or not," I joked.

"Well, of course I don't." He thought I was serious. "They don't sell rubbers in the commissary," he added.

"There's a condom dispenser in the men's room at most gas stations," I advised, "but you really don't need one. I was just kidding you. Whoever you get laid by will squirt some stuff in the end of your dick when it's all over, and you won't have to worry a lick."

"What kind of stuff?"

"Hell Squid, I don't know what they call it, but it works."

"So you're telling me that I can't catch anything."

"Right!"

"How do you know all this shit?"

"Once you go through it, you'll know it too."

Squid concurred that Saturday would be the best day to head to the County Line. Friday evening we had a big football game at Kane Field against our rival, Southside High School, and we couldn't miss that. After the game we would check out for the weekend and drive over to my house. Saturday afternoon we would head back to the south side and pick up Brad and Zebra. Zebra got his name because he had a couple of weird abnormal white stripes through his black hair. His real name was Boris Kowalski. He was from Boston. Zebra, Brad, Squid, and I would then head to the County Line. Squid thought it would be a lot safer going during the daylight hours, so we agreed to do that.

After the sun came up on Friday morning, and we could see the football field, we couldn't believe our eyes. In huge capital letters right on the field it said, "FUCK KANE." The whole school was irate, cadets and faculty. Whoever did it, and we know who did it, will be sorry. They had broken into the shed where the lime and lime dispenser were kept. The lime was used for the ten yard stripes and end zone hash on the football field and also to stripe the foul lines and outline the batter's boxes, on-deck circles, and coaches' boxes on the baseball diamond. By the light of the moon those despicable assholes lettered our field. Major Hard-ass took immediate steps to wash the lime out before the crowd arrived later in the day, but you could still tell what it said at kickoff time. A meeting took place later Friday afternoon in our smoking lounge in which Squid and I were very involved. It was the first discussion about how we were going to retaliate.

It was mandatory for all cadets to wear our uniforms to all sporting events, so we couldn't change until after the game, just prior to checking out. Well, let me tell you, their fans laughed at the lettering on the field, and that pissed us off. Then we lost the game 21-20, and that pissed us off even more. We vowed that we would get even.

It was late when we got to my house, and neither Squid nor I had eaten much, so we raided the refrigerator for a midnight snack. We were tired, so after we filled our gut we crashed.

Saturday morning I slept in a little, and then headed down to the kitchen. Squid was there eating some breakfast that Susan had prepared for him. "Massa Dean, what would you like for breakfast," she asked. It was always, Mister Bass, Mrs. Bass, Master Dean and Miss Carrie, and yes sir and yes ma'am. Susan always showed respect, and she was a fine cook, so we enjoyed having her around. Actually, she sewed pretty well too. After Squid and I got our promotions, she sewed the corporal stripes on all our shirts and jackets. Susan always called him Master Marvin, she wouldn't call him Master Squid. I noticed that Squid was eating a small steak with his eggs, so I asked Susan if she had another thawed out. "Ain't we always got some thawed out? You knows yo' father likes his steaks, so I always has some thawed out and ready to go," she replied. Susan often butchered pronunciation of the English language.

"Where's Tina," I asked.

"She's helpin' yo' sister redecorate her room," claimed Susan. "They had their breakfast mor'an two hours ago."

Carrie just turned 17. She was a junior at Robert E. Lee High School, and one of their cheerleaders. On certain holidays, when Lee's band was in a parade, Carrie would fix it so I could drive Mom's silver Cadillac convertible with the cheerleaders sitting all over it. We would always ride in front, ahead of the majorettes and band. Squid thought that Carrie was gorgeous. Early in our senior year he wanted me to fix him up with her. I told him, "No way!" He never questioned me as to why I said that. Subsequently, however, they did get "thrown" together many times.

Tina was a fox, and a sexy one at that. She was a hard worker and also very respectful. Tina was about ten years older than me, and when nobody was around she would talk some shit with me. I often thought that she would crawl under the covers with me if I asked her.

By the time we had finished breakfast and yakked for a while it was past eleven. I poked my head into Carrie's room to say hello to her and Tina, then Squid and I took off.

Once we got back to the south side, we picked up Brad and Zebra. Time was getting close and Squid was getting more nervous then ever.

"What if we get arrested at County Line?" Squid wanted to know.

"I'll come bail you out." said Zebra.

"How can you bail me out if you're in jail too?" asked Squid.

"Hell, they have to give you one phone call. Call your dad, he'll bail you out," said Brad.

"My dad's in Miami, he can't bail me out," stated Squid. "This is something to seriously consider. Don't you think so?"

"Don't worry about it," said Zebra. "The chance of something like that happening is very remote."

"Remote, remote, so you agree it could happen, right?" said Squid.

"You worry too much," I said laughing. "If something goes wrong and you get locked up, I'll take care of Granny's ashes for you."

Squid did not seem amused. "By the way," he asked, "have you guys ever been to a whore house before? Huh, Brad? Huh, Zebra?" The three of us howled with laughter.

"Hey Squid, drive by Southside High on the way." I requested. "I want to take a closer look at that place."

"How's looking at an empty school on a Saturday going to help?" he asked.

"I don't know, just drive by and let me look." We did, and then headed to the County Line.

We pulled up in front of the truck stop, but Squid wouldn't cut off the engine. "What's the matter, Squid? asked Brad.

"Aren't you guys hungry? Let's go eat lunch before we do this."

"Damn Squid, we had breakfast just two hours ago. Stop stalling, go on in." I said.

"Why are there so many cars here? I don't see anybody around." observed Squid.

"They're all in the trailers, getting laid, like you're going to be," said Zebra.

"Wait a minute, you guys, I'm not the only one going in there. Aren't we all going to do this?" retorted Squid.

"You're the virgin, Squid. We are here to get you laid." claimed Zebra.

"You guys are chicken. You want me to do this by myself." Squid turned to Zebra and asked, "How do I know you and Brad aren't virgins? Prove that you're not virgins."

"You're just stalling," said Brad. "Do you want to get laid or not?"

"Yes, right after lunch. Maybe some of these cars will have cleared out," said Squid.

"Okay, let's go get some Krystals and then come back," conceded Brad.

"Okay."

We headed to the nearest Krystal. Each of us gobbled about eight of their little burgers. During lunch our discussion continued.

"Are you serious about waiting out in the car while I go in?" asked Squid.

"Squid, we are all here to give you moral support, not to get laid ourselves," said Brad.

Brad, Zebra and I were sure that Squid would not go in unless we accompanied him, so we decided that all four of us would go get laid. That made Squid so happy that when we pulled back into a parking place at the County Line, he shut off his engine immediately. There were still a lot of cars at the truck stop, but we got out of the car and walked inside. There was one big, mean looking fellow behind the counter, and not another soul in sight. We approached him.

"We would like to visit with four of your girls, if it's alright with you," said Brad.

"How old are you boys? You look damned young to me," roared the man in a gruff voice.

"How old do we need to be to visit your girls?" asked Brad.

"21," was his answer.

"Well hell, we're all 21," responded Brad.

"All right, if you say so. I don't want to get in any trouble for letting minors through my gate back there. Do you under-stand?"

"Yes sir, we understand."

"Go around the right side of the building and I'll buzz you through the gate. Two of you go to trailer 4, one to trailer 8, and the other to 9," he explained.

"Where do we pay?" asked Squid.

"You pay your girl based on the services she performs. Do you have plenty of money?"

"I think so," said Squid. "Do you give S&H green stamps?"

"No! I'm setting the buzzer for the gate. It will automatically shut off when you close the gate on the other side. Okay?"

"Okay, but how do we get out?" asked Squid.

"As long as you have paid for your services, your girl will buzz you out. Now get going."

"Yes sir!"

We went around the right side of the building, as instructed. "Hey Squid," I said, "we should have a couple of Dick Tracy's two-way wrist radios. That way I could talk you through this thing." He grinned nervously.

There was a tall chain link fence, with barbed wire on top, surrounding all of the trailers. As we got near the buzzing gate, we stopped in our tracks. Right in front of us, on the inside of the gate, stood two large, mean looking Doberman pinchers. They were standing there like statues just staring at us. They weren't growling, but they were showing their teeth. Like a silent snarl. We stood there, also like statues, staring back.

"Damn, those dogs look like they could tear your leg off," said Zebra.

"I am not sure I want to lose my virginity bad enough to risk tangling with those dogs," said Squid, as the gate kept buzzing.

"Man, those are Dobermans," said Brad. "They are the meanest dogs on the planet."

"Maybe this isn't such a good idea," I said.

Finally, Brad reached over and opened the gate about two inches, then closed it quickly so the buzzing would stop. The Dobermans didn't move a muscle. The four of us turned around and headed to Squid's car, as we all looked over our shoulders.

"Well hell," said I, "we need to find another way to get Squid laid." But that was it for the County Line, at least for the time being.

What a let-down. We had been talking about going to the County Line for a year, and all of a sudden it just fizzled out.

Poor Squid, sometimes he has pitiful luck. Sunday night

we checked back in at school. After taps sounded, everybody crawled into their bunks. Everybody, that is, except for Squid. He tried, but his feet only went half way under his top sheet. Someone had short-sheeted his bed. Let me explain how that works. All cadets make up their beds every morning. The top sheet is double folded over the blanket just below where the pillow sits. Hospital corners are required on all corners of the sheets and blanket. They have to be so tight that the inspecting officer can bounce a quarter on your blanket, much like a trampoline. Well, somebody undid Squids top sheet at the bottom, then folded it in half, tucking it with hospital corners at the pillow end. When he tried to slide into bed, he could only go part way.

"Shit!" he said. "Now I have to remake my bed."

CHAPTER FIVE

Squid Makes Headlines

I was reading a book entitled *Medieval Archery*, two nights later as Squid and I sat at our desk during study period. I was fairly good at the sport and had several bows and many arrows. Squid was reading a *Dick Tracy* comic.

"Hey Deano," he said, "Your flattop looks like the one on this miserable character that Tracy is chasing after. In fact his name is Flattop."

"Let me see," I said, "Hell, he doesn't look anything like me, nor does his flattop."

"Well, you're both ugly, and you both have flattops."

"Hey Squid, this archery book gives me an idea of how we can strike back at Southside."

"How's that?"

"Well, pay attention now, this is involved."

"Okay, I'm listening," said Squid.

"You guys own a fleet of charters so you can relate to this. What if we shot a couple of arrows, with light fishing lines attached to them, over the top of their school building? To the light lines we will tie heavy lines, maybe even wire lines, like the deep line you use on your boats. We will send a couple of guys around the building to pull the light lines over the top. Attached to the heaviest lines will be rolls of insulation soaked in green and gold paint. As the lines are pulled from the other side of the building the insulation will stripe their building, and their roof, with Kane colors. It will take forever for them to get rid of it, and it will teach them not to fuck with Kane Military. What do you think?"

"Ingenious!" said Squid, "But too elaborate and very risky."

"How so?"

"Well, for starters, what if the police catch us doing it. It will take some time to soak the insulation in paint, and then drag it over the building. They patrol around schools all the time. It's too risky. If they catch us, they would put us in jail for destruction of public property, and we would flunk out of school because we wouldn't be able to go to class. Or, we would flunk because Hard-ass would probably expel us, and our parents would disown us because they would lose a ton of money, and-"

"Okay, okay, stop," said I. "We'll figure a way where we won't get caught."

"Like you figured a way to get me laid," he stated sarcastically.

"Touché, we'll come up with some way to solve both problems," I said. "Say have you ever opened the box that contains Granny's ashes, and looked inside."

"God no, why would I want to do that?"

"I don't know. I was just wondering."

It was Tuesday, exactly one week since Squid mailed his silver brick to the police department. He wondered if someone actually sat there and pulled out all of the staples. He got his answer that day when a police car pulled up on Hard-ass Circle. The officer went to Major Harden's office, and the major then accompanied the officer to Miss Mary Ann's 4th period English class, where Squid and I were both in attendance. Major Harden stepped into the classroom and asked for Marvin Brennan. Squid stood up and walked out. The officer put Squid's hands behind his back, and then handcuffed him. Squid was escorted to the patrol car, put in the back seat, and the cop drove off. I had a good idea what it was all about, but didn't want to say anything to anybody.

They took Squid down to the police station, unhandcuffed him, and then rehandcuffed him with his hands in front. They took his mug shot and fingerprinted him. Then they sat him down at a table with his silver brick and a staple remover. While Squid was pulling those staples out one by one, with his handcuffs still on, a photographer came in and took his picture. Once all of the staples were removed, Squid got a lecture, and they returned him to Franklin Hall.

Squid's picture was on the front page of Wednesday's *Florida Times-Union*, Jacksonville's morning newspaper. The caption below the photo was a play on words. It read: "Stapilization of Currency," and then explained who, when, and why in a short article. The article never mentioned Kane Military Academy, but it didn't have to, because Squid was wearing his uniform and anyone could tell he was a Kane cadet. Naturally,

Squid had a lot of explaining to do to Major Harden. Oddly enough, the major didn't mandate Bull Ring. I guess he figured that Squid had already learned his lesson. Squid bought every newspaper in the rack outside the smoking lounge. He was so proud, that he mailed off several copies, and carried the article in his pocket to show everyone.

"Geez, was that an ordeal," said Squid. "Have you ever ridden in the back seat of a police car with your hands handcuffed behind you? It is incredibly uncomfortable."

CHAPTER SIX

Lifesaving

It rained on Thursday, so we had our drill inside the indoor swimming center. It was a life saving drill that I was dreading, because I didn't swim very well. Lt. Bones Gifford was a certified life guard, so he was the only cadet allowed to instruct the drill without a faculty member present. Each of the cadets had their swim trunks on under their uniform trousers, and we were wearing tee shirts and tennis shoes and socks. We each had to jump into the pool individually, remove our tennis shoes, socks, and trousers while treading water. Then we had to tie a knot at the bottom of each trouser leg, close the fly, then swing the trousers through the air, catching air as they hit the water, thus making a floatation device out of our trousers. It seemed like a really dumb drill, because the trousers wouldn't hold air very long. After completing the maneuver we had to dive to the bottom of the pool to retrieve our shoes and socks. I made it through the process, but did so with a little difficulty.

Squid had a fellow in his squad named Private Ronald Beckum. Beckum claimed he couldn't swim. He was in tears and freaking out, but Gifford seemed to ignore him.

"God, don't make me jump into the pool," Beckum cried. "I can't swim a lick. I will drown and you will have my death on your hands. It will haunt you the rest of your life. If I jump in, I will sink like an anchor. God, don't make me do it."

Gifford walked up to Beckum and said, "Learn to swim!" then pushed him into the pool. Beckum went straight to the bottom in a panic.

Squid, who was a great swimmer, turned to Gifford and said, "You dumb shit!" then dove to the bottom of the pool. Beckum was a big guy and Squid had problems pulling him out. Beckum had taken in some water, had passed out, and wasn't breathing. Squid gave Beckum mouth-to-mouth resuscitation until he responded. Two other cadets dashed over to the infirmary and brought back a stretcher and a nurse. Beckum was put on the stretcher and taken to the infirmary. Once more Squid turned to

Gifford and said, "You dumb shit!"

"I am going to write you up for insubordination to an officer," snapped Gifford.

Squid spun around and hit Gifford with a great punch, knocking him into the pool. Bones Gifford climbed out of the pool with blood running from his nose. He dismissed the platoon, and as he walked out of the swim center he said, "You've had it Brennan!"

Gifford did as he said he would do. He wrote up Squid for insubordination. The following afternoon there was a hearing in Major Harden's office. Besides Gifford and Squid, Brad and I, and the other two squad leaders were all required to attend. After about an hour of discussion, Major Harden looked at Gifford and severely scolded him. He dropped the insubordination charge against Squid, and praised him for his quick response. Before we left Harden's office the major asked, "Why does everybody call you Squid?" Squid explained that his dad owned a fleet of charter fishing boats in Miami, and that was the reason why he was a good swimmer.

During one of our formations, a week later, Squid was presented with a life saving medal to wear on his dress uniform.

It was Friday afternoon and I was ready to check out. Linda and I had not seen each other in nearly two weeks, so we were anxious. Squid stayed on campus, and I took off in the turdmobile. I picked Linda up about 7 p.m. It was an unseasonably warm evening so we grabbed a blanket and headed to the beach. We decided to go to an isolated spot that we had been to before. The moon was full and the ocean was at low tide. We rolled the blanket out on the sand and made fantastic love to music from a new transistor radio that I had recently purchased. Then we just laid there watching the moon, and the moon's reflection on the rolling surf. Even though Linda is a little prissy, I still enjoy being with her. We sat on the blanket and talked about a number of subjects. One topic was the panty raid that a bunch of us cadets were going to make on Hobart, and how she was going to help make it successful. Our conversation soon swung to Squid.

"I told you that Squid is a virgin, right?"

"Right!"

"We need to get him laid."

"Okay."

"Do you have any ideas on how we can accomplish that?"

"Sure, take him to a whore house," she said. I couldn't believe my ears. Linda was so finicky, I couldn't imagine her saying that. I had been afraid to mention that option. Well, I still didn't mention it. "Of course, if you did," she added, "you would wait out front, right?"

"Oh, right, absolutely!"

We strolled down to the water's edge and walked in the surf.

"Do you know any really loose girls at Hobart that would jump his bones?" I asked.

"Most of the girls that live at Hobart are horny and sex-starved."

"But, do you know one that would take the initiative and score with him? Squid doesn't know how to make the first move, so we need a girl that will lead him through it."

"I have a couple of girls in mind. Let me talk to them and I'll try to line up something definite for Squid." Linda's long blonde hair glistened in the moonlight.

"That would be great. Just let me know."

"I'll talk to them this week," she added.

It was getting late. I took Linda to her house and kissed her goodnight, then pointed the turdmobile in the direction of home. I was less then two miles from my house when there was a terrible noise under the car, and it quit running. I coasted across the shoulder of the road and into the edge of a vacant lot. It was late, and I was not going to try to figure out what went wrong. I put the emergency brake on, not that it mattered, and hoofed it the rest of the way to the house. I was really tired, and when my head hit the pillow I was immediately asleep.

CHAPTER SEVEN

Smokin' Tailpipes

At breakfast Saturday morning, I told Dad and Mom about my car. Mom came to my rescue right away. "Oh honey," she addressed Dad, "Dean has been driving that old car ever since he got his learners permit. Don't you think it's time to get him something more reliable?"

"Dean, how much money do you have in the bank from your summer job?" asked Dad.

I told him, and Mom was on my side again, "Oh, let Dean keep his hard earned money, we can get him a newer car, besides it's his birthday." It was music to my ears.

"Go down to Marlin Chrysler-Plymouth and see Homer Handley." said Dad, "Tell him you're my son. He is the new car general manager, and an old friend. Their used car lot is adjacent to the new car showroom, and he can help you with any vehicle they have. Tell him you want to trade your Olds, but that it needs repair. Also, tell him where it is so he can send someone out to look at it. Take the Pontiac. I won't need it today. Call me later and fill me in on the options."

"Yes sir!" I said, "Thank you sir." I was tickled to death with the thought of getting rid of the turdmobile, and also elated that I could drive Dad's new two-tone 1955 Pontiac Star Chief Custom Catalina with its Over Head Valve 180 Horsepower V-8. It was the car that he drove to work each day. Dad never let me drive his Kaiser Darrin, his two-seat sports car with doors that would slide forward into the fenders and a three-position convertible top. Kaiser only built 435 Kaiser Darrin automobiles in 1954, its only year of production. It was Dad's pride and joy. He wouldn't even let Mom drive it.

"While you are looking at cars, Dean, give me your thoughts on what we might get Carrie. We have promised to get her a car, and should probably do it soon."

"By the way, where is Carrie?" I asked.

"She and some of her friends are having a pajama party over at Sharon's house," said Mom. Carrie's friend Sharon was a real looker. In fact, she had won a big teenage beauty pageant a few months earlier. Maybe we should have a pajama raid, I thought.

I thanked Dad and Mom, got the Pontiac keys, and took off for the Marlin dealership. I hoped that I could find a Ford or Chevy on their used car lot. Chrysler products had been so ugly through 1954, and Chrysler knew it, so they hired some of the designers away from Studebaker. The 1955 models that those guys designed for Chrysler were very sharp, and compared favorably with anything that Ford or GM had to offer.

I entered the showroom and asked a salesman if Homer Handley was in. He indicated that I should take the stairs to the second floor, and that his office was the first door on the left. When Mr. Handley found out that I was Dad's son, he bent over backwards for me. Dad seemed to have connections everywhere. Mr. Handley walked me over to the used car lot and showed me several vehicles that I wasn't very impressed with. Then we walked back to the new car showroom, where he showed me a new Plymouth Belvedere with a four-barrel carb and dual exhausts. He said, "This car, with its power-pack, will out-perform any stock automobile on the road today." I stood there visualizing what that Plymouth would look like with the hood and trunk chrome removed, the side trim changed, mercury skirts, assimilated wire wheels, and a new custom paint job. It really looked good in my mind. I told Homer Handley that Dad wanted me to look at used cars not new ones. He laughed and said, "I have sent somebody out to appraise your Oldsmobile. We always offer a higher trade in allowance on a new vehicle, and with the discounts that I can give you there wouldn't be all that much difference. Let me talk to your dad." Well, to make a long story short, Mr. Handley put a great deal together, called Dad and convinced him, then sent the paperwork to our house for Dad to sign, and handed me the keys. While all this was happening, I called my friend Rooney at his custom shop to get a rough price on having the Plymouth customized. A little later, I called him back to let him know that I was bringing the car to him. Being a friend, he gave me a super deal that would only dent my savings account. I left the car with him and he drove me back to Marlin Chrysler-Plymouth so I could pick up Dad's Pontiac. Marlin's tow truck hauled the turdmobile away. I never saw it again.

I explained to Dad that they had to do some work on the Plymouth, and that I would go get it next weekend. He let me take the Pontiac Saturday night so I could take Linda out on my birthday. I had to promise him that I wouldn't drive all over town. Linda and I went to a movie theater to see *Mister Roberts* with Henry Fonda, James Cagney and Jack Lemmon. What a good movie, I thought. What a great weekend I also thought. On our way back to Linda's house, the car radio rocked with Elvis Presley's release on the Sun record label, *That's All Right.*

"I really want to see Elvis Presley again," said Linda, "I love his style."

"Yep, I'd like to see him again too." We had attended one of his concerts just three months earlier, in late July.

"Will he come back to town?"

"I'm sure he will, sometime."

"That would be so neat."

"Say, don't forget to talk to those girls at Hobart about helping Squid lose his virginity."

"I won't forget," she said, then added, "I have to go to Ocala with my folks next weekend, so I won't be able to see you."

"That's a bummer, I'll miss you, and I'm anxious for you to see my new car."

"I can't wait to see it either," she said. "What a neat birthday present."

Dad drove me back to Kane late Sunday, because I had no wheels.

CHAPTER EIGHT

How to Score

Squid sat next to me in 4th period English, about three rows from the front. I leaned over, and in a whisper I asked him, "Do you think she is wearing her skirts shorter?"

"Looks shorter to me," he whispered back.

"Damn she is getting sexier all the time."

"I know it. I would sure like some of that."

"You wouldn't know what to do with it if you did have it," I said.

Miss Mary Ann looked back at us and asked, "Is your conversation something you would like to share with the rest of the class?"

"Actually, I was just commenting to Corporal Brennan on how attractive you looked today, Miss Mary Ann." I could tell she blushed.

"Flattery will not help your grade at all Corporal Bass, but thank you." she said.

When the bell sounded to end the period, Miss Mary Ann said, "Corporal Bass would you mind staying just a moment?" After everyone had left the room she walked around in front of her desk, then eased into a sitting position on top of the desk and crossed her legs. Her skirt inched higher then I had ever seen it. She said, "Corporal Bass, this is a strict institution. Please don't comment in class on how I look, what I am wearing, or the like. Do you understand?"

"Yes ma'am, but I only meant it as a compliment. You are a beautiful lady, if I were your age, or you were my age, I would ask you out."

She really blushed this time, but stated, "Corporal Bass, you are an attractive young man, and if I were your age, or you were my age, I would probably accept. Now get out of here."

"Yes ma'am, thank you ma'am, good b-bye." I stuttered. As I walked through the door I glanced over my shoulder and she was still sitting on the desk with her legs crossed.

Squid was waiting outside, "What was that all about?" he

asked.

"Hell, I don't know, she just didn't want me to compliment her in class."

"Was that all?"

"I don't know. I don't know whether there was anything more to it than that." I then told
Squid exactly what we each had said.

"Shit," he said, "sounds like she wants to get chummy."

"No, no, no, just forget this whole conversation Squid, okay?"

"If you say so."

I asked Squid to forget it, but I sure couldn't forget it. I thought about her words over and over. Then I would wonder, and try to read something into it. Then I'd read it back out.

That evening during study period I guess I was exceptionally quiet. I sat there shining my black shoes, glossing them with a little bay rum, and then started to work on my brass belt buckle.

"You are quieter than this guy Mumbles that Tracy is after," said Squid with his head buried in another *Dick Tracy* comic book. "You must be thinking about Miss Boobs."

"I told you to forget it, and don't call her that."

"What do you mean, don't call her that?" he said, "you have been calling her that since we have known her."

"I know, I'm sorry. She's a pretty cool lady."

"She is stacked better'n a brick shithouse."

"Cool it Squid!"

"Man, I can tell where your mind is," said Squid. "Hey, do me a favor."

"What?"

"I taught you how to study, or rather how to make good grades without studying, so teach me how to be successful with chicks. I mean, you never have a problem scoring with girls. What is your secret?"

"Hell Squid, it's because I'm so irresistible."

"Seriously Deano, help me out."

"Well, first of all, don't ask a girl out on a date unless she is good looking. If you ask out an ugly girl, you will set a precedent, and you will screw up your reputation. Girls with huge tits usually have a huge ass. Girls with little tits usually have a little ass. Only date those with a nice figure. It is important to have a good looking dame at your side. Sometimes the gorgeous ones are more apt to say 'yes.'

"Why?"

"Because most of the guys think they are untouchable, or they assume they would have no chance with someone so good looking. Often, the best looking girls are asked out less than the ones with average looks. My point is, keep your standards high."

"That sounds like bull shit!"

"I'm serious Squid. Furthermore, girls are generally more bashful than guys. It is important that you get on the right track sexually from the beginning of a relationship. Discuss sex immediately with your date. Let her know where you stand. If she isn't interested in talking about it, the chances are she isn't going to be interested in doing it. Guys need to take the initiative when it comes to certain things. Remember, girls like sex just as much as guys do, but they are not as apt to bring up the subject initially. Guys are more goal-oriented, whereas chicks have a tendency to be a little more reluctant. You are very tentative with women, Squid. You have to take the bull by the horns, or you will never get laid."

"Think so?"

"Know so! Also, girls are more sensitive and emotional than guys are. Girls cry when things don't go right, or when they are hurt about something. And, they can be hurt easily. A guy will usually just let things roll off his back, so to speak. If you are insensitive to a girl's plight, you will not score many points with her. It is important that she thinks you care about whatever difficulties she is facing and feeling. In other words, be sympathetic of her predicament, whatever it may be, even if you believe that the matter is trivial.

Little things are much more important to girls, than to guys. Buy her stuff. Little things mean a lot. Flowers tell her you care.   Red roses tell her you really care.   Cards for special occasions, or for no reason at all, will let her know that you're thinking about her. This goes back to my point that chicks are more sensitive. You will get more mileage out of doing the little things. Courtesy is important. Always be a gentleman, whether you are with a lady or a prostitute. Open their car door for them. Actually, open any door for them. When you are walking along a sidewalk with a girl, always walk on the curb side.

"Why walk on the curb side?"

"Shit Squid, it's an old custom that goes back to the days when ladies wore long skirts. By walking on the curb side a guy was protecting his lady from being splashed by a passing carriage, or later by a passing automobile. It just shows that he is a gentleman. And, a lady likes a gentleman. It is important that you treat any female properly, especially your girlfriends mother. Speaking of mothers, whenever you get serious about a chick take a good look at her mother, because more often than not the chick is going to turn out to be a lot like her mother."

"How do you know that?"

"Dad told me that a long time ago. After he said that, I started comparing girls to their mothers, and it is true. They really do turn out like their mothers most of the time."

"Really?" said Squid. "What else?"

"Wheels are paramount to some chicks. They would much rather be riding around in a classy looking car than in a rattletrap. Your car is only one year old, so you're in good shape when it comes to that. Sometimes, the real quality girls could care less. I'm talking about the ones that get into you for who you are, not for your wheels or your money. With those girls, a classy car is just icing on the cake. Prior to ordering my new car I drove my nine year old turdmobile, and even though she is prissy, Linda couldn't have given a shit. Your wardrobe is important, but it is relative to whom you are, who she is, and the image you want to convey. Biker broads like guys with tattoos, in leather and chains. Classy chicks like collared shirts, tucked in, with a nice belt and great looking shoes. They also like uniforms."

"What else?"

"Girls like a commitment. Security is important. They all want to be going steady with a cool guy. If you are cool, you have no problem. Just learn to take the initiative, Squid, and you will be fine."

We had two more discussions in the smoking lounge on

how to get back at Southside High, but no firm plans were made. I still liked my bow and arrow idea.

One wall of the smoking lounge was all French doors, with small panes of glass. One evening, Tommy, Squid's old room-mate was pissed off about something and he decided to take his wrath out on the glass. Tommy put his right fist through six panes before blood started running everywhere. He couldn't write for three weeks.

Along the inside corridor near the smoking lounge was a bank of twelve pay phones. There was always a mob around the pay phones because those phones were the only way for cadets to call out. Those making calls lined up with their nickels. New cadets had a real problem because they could get bumped in line by anyone that outranked them. Receiving calls was nearly impossible. Anyone calling a cadet would have to keep dialing those numbers until they lucked out and got a phone to ring between all of the outgoing calls. Even then, if the cadet receiving the call wasn't nearby, or in the smoking lounge, forget it, because nobody was going to check rooms, and the school hadn't installed a loud speaker system as yet. The situation at Hobart was very similar, so Linda and I hardly ever tried to speak with each other during the week.

I was able to get one call out, to my friend Rooney, to find out how my new car was coming along. To my disappointment, he said he needed it another week, but that it was looking great. So, I asked Squid to check out and head home with me, because otherwise I would have to rely on my Dad for transportation. It was a good weekend for Squid to come over too, because Linda was going to be in Ocala.

"Sure," indicated Squid. "I was going to take care of Granny's ashes this weekend, but that can wait." Squid was always pleased to visit my house anytime. One of the reasons was my sister, Carrie. Although he never would admit it, Squid had an obvious crush on her.

CHAPTER NINE

New Boys

Prior to checking out for the weekend, Zebra and I were down by the main lounge where all the non-smokers congregated. We cornered Artie Mann, who was one of the new boys.

"Recruit Mann," Zebra asked, "Where are you from?"

"I live here, but I grew up in Ozark, Arkansas, Sir!"

"Ozark, Arkansas. Do they have electricity there?" I inquired.

"Oh, yes Sir," stated Artie.

"Did they teach you to read in school?" I asked.

"Yes Sir, I know how to read."

"Being from Arkansas, you should know what horse shit looks like. Right?" queried Zebra.

"Yes Sir, I do," replied Artie.

"Recruit Mann, we want you to obtain four water pails full of horse shit, filled to the very top, and have them sitting underneath the north bleachers by 1600 hours (4 p.m.) this Sunday, or else," I instructed.

"Yes Sir. I will do it, Sir."

Artie knew what the "or else" might entail, so we were sure the filled buckets would be there when we checked in Sunday afternoon.

Squid and I decided that we would go down to Bay Street to play billiards at Andy's Billiard Parlor. True billiards is played on a table with no pockets and only three balls. If the white ball is your cue ball, then the white ball with the red dot is mine. Sometimes the second cue ball is yellow. The third ball is red. Scoring is accomplished by hitting the other two balls in combination with a rail.

Bay Street was notorious, and was always jumping on a Friday night. It was filled with tattoo parlors, bars, Gypsies telling fortunes, pool halls and prostitutes. There were so many prostitutes that they would sit on the window sills of many second floor windows, clad in scanty garb, whistling at the men that walked by. The ones that weren't in the windows were either plying their trade or walking the sidewalks looking for business. Andy's Billiard Parlor was an upstairs establishment. We parked Squid's Ford, and climbed the narrow stairs to Andy's. After shooting several games of billiards and snooker, we left and climbed back into Squid's car. We had just pulled out of our parking place and were nearing the corner when one of the hookers flagged us down. "Stop the car," I said as I rolled my window down. She stepped right up to the open window, and bent over so she could see Squid on the driver's side. She was wearing no bra, and her boobs were so big that I could see her belly button between them. It suddenly occurred to me that we could get Squid laid, right here, right now.

"Hi honey," I said, "Are you interested in making a little money?"

"Sure baby, I'll do anything for 20 dollars. Are you the one that's going to get it on with me?" she asked.

"No, I need for you to give your first class treatment to my friend here behind the wheel."
I had no longer gotten those words out of my mouth when Squid popped the clutch and squealed
out, almost taking that poor girls head off.

"Damn Deano, speak for yourself, I am not going to go into one of those scroungy, nasty, scummy pads with some girl who is probably a walking clap factory."

"Hell Squid, we were just in one of those scroungy, nasty, scummy places shooting billiards. It wouldn't be much different."
"Besides, I don't have a rubber, and she probably doesn't have
any of that stuff you were telling me about, that you squirt in a dick, so hell no, this isn't the time or the place."

"Oh well, forget that I mentioned it."

Saturday morning, Susan was fixing breakfast for Carrie, Squid, Tina and I. We had a large breakfast room adjacent to the kitchen. Squid was flirting with Carrie, but she never seemed very interested in him. The thought crossed my mind that maybe just maybe I could get Tina to take him down. To the girls I said, "I tried to get my virgin friend here laid last night but he would have none of it."

I didn't see Susan standing behind me. "Massa Dean, oh Massa Dean, you is goin' to get that fine boy, Massa Marvin, into a heap of trouble." We couldn't help it, but all four of us broke out in laughter.

Tina looked at Squid with a grin on her face, "Are you really a virgin?"

"Well if Deano, er Dean, had anything to do about it I wouldn't be. That's for sure."

Still grinning Tina said, "I lost my virginity when I was 13."

I said, "I'd like to hear that story sometime."

"Remind me later, and I'll tell it to you sometime." she said, still grinning.

"Susan is right, Dean, you are bad." said Carrie.

"Hush Carrie, I can tell a story or two about you, but I won't."

"You better never!"

As soon as Squid and I left the house, the first thing out of his mouth was, "Is Carrie a virgin?"

"Probably," I said, but I lied. Carrie thought she had the house to herself on Labor Day weekend, so she invited her friend Sharon, who had a car, over for the long weekend. Mom and Dad were out of town. Tina, who was visiting her sister, and Susan both had the weekend off. I had gone to Daytona Beach, but drove back to Jacksonville early Sunday morning. Obviously a day earlier then the girls expected me, because I caught them shacked up in two rooms with a couple of guys from Lee High. As I topped the stairs Carrie's door was closed, but I had to pass a guest room on the way to my room. There was Sharon, naked as the day she was born, and some fellow. I reached around and knocked on the open door, and Sharon let out a shrill scream. When Carrie heard it she bolted from her room. Well, I ran the guys off, and then had a late breakfast with Carrie and Sharon. They blushed with embarrassment.

While we were sitting at the breakfast table, I ribbed Sharon, "You look absolutely ravishing naked." Her blush reddened even more. Anyway, that's how I knew that Carrie, and for that matter Sharon, were not virgins. Carrie told me the next day that Sharon wanted to go out with me. I reminded Carrie that Linda was my girlfriend.

Squid's mind was on Carrie as we drove away from the

house, but for the moment mine was on Tina. Tina's day off is on Monday. I wondered what she did on her day off.

We stopped at a Pure Oil station to gas up, collected our S&H green stamps, and then went over to Rooney's shop to see how my car was progressing. The body work was done, and primed, and the car was awaiting its new paint job. The merc skirts were also primed and hung nearby all prepped for paint. I told Rooney that everything looked good. He indicated that the car would be ready about Thursday. I told him that I would pick it up Saturday.

There was only one speed shop in Jacksonville, so that was our next stop. I wanted to soup up my new car to its max, to assure that it would outrun anything in town. I got a few great ideas from the boys there. My buddy, Ray, who was a freshman at the University of Florida in Gainesville, had a Corvette with a hole in the hood, and a Pontiac engine popping out. It was fast, and I especially wanted the capability to whip him. After we left the speed shop we stopped by Marlin Chrysler-Plymouth to pick up a cardboard box full of the stuff I had left in the turdmobile. The doggie knob that was attached to my steering wheel wasn't in the box. When I inquired about it, they apologized and indicated that my Oldsmobile had already gone to the salvage yard. I guess I would just have to go buy another doggie knob. How else could I drive with my right arm around Linda and a can of beer in my left hand?

Linda called from Ocala at dinner time. "I have some news for you," she said. "I have Squid fixed up with a girl named Wanda for Friday night. She said she has never broken in a virgin so she is looking forward to it. Is that okay?"

"That is perfect, he will finally get laid. Good work doll!"

We talked for about 20 minutes, gave each other our love then hung up. I told Squid about the date Friday night, and what Wanda had said to Linda. He smiled and asked, "Do I need to wear a rubber?"

"Unless you want to get her pregnant," I said.

"Let's stop and get some on our way to school tomorrow."

"Okay." Squid and I spent a quiet Saturday evening at the house, playing chess. Sunday we fooled around with my throwing knives and axes, and then returned to Kane in the afternoon.

It was after 4 p.m. when we checked back in. Squid and I walked over to the north bleachers. Sure enough, there were four pails of horse shit sitting there. We found Zebra and Crawfish, who were the other two squad leaders in our platoon, then rounded up 12 new boys, including Artie Mann, and marched them down to the field that lay just beyond the baseball diamond. None of them were from our platoon.

"Recruit Mann, take one new boy with you, get those four buckets and take them over to the hose by the shed, add some water, then bring them here." ordered Squid.

"Yes sir," responded Mann, and he did.

"Okay now," I said, "spread that shit out into a square about 10 feet by 10 feet."

"Yes sir, how should we spread it?"

"You don't have a shovel, so spread it with your feet."

"Sir, we all have our uniforms on and our shoes are shined for mess formation."

"My heart bleeds for you," said Crawfish.

"Please Corporal Crawford, don't make us do this."

"Do as we ordered, immediately, or you can spread it with your noses while on your hands and knees," said Squid.

"Yes sir, we'll spread it with our feet." The new boys turned the pails over, and did a remarkable job of molding it into a 10 foot by 10 foot square.

"Okay," I said, "I want three columns of four men each. Do it now."

Squid took over at that point. "Right face, forward march." He marched them through the 10 foot square. "To the rear, march. To the rear, march. To the rear, march." Over and over, for more than five minutes he marched them back and forth, until their shoes and the bottoms of their uniform trousers were totally covered with the material from those pails. "Detail halt." He stopped them right in the middle of the square. "Now listen carefully, men. We are going to head back to Franklin Hall. You will remain at attention, in this square, until you hear the bugle for mess, in about five minutes. You may then dismiss yourselves and run to mess formation. You will not under any circumstances mention any of our names in connection with this escapade. If that happens, your punishment will be severe. Do you understand?"

"Yes sir," they responded. We had just enough time to head back to our rooms, buff our shoes, and wipe a little Brasso on and off our belt buckles, before the bugle sounded. Brasso was a new product, and it was great. My first year at KMA, we had to clean our brass with a blitz cloth. A blitz cloth would clean the brass, but would leave a film on our buckles.

Needless to say, nobody would get near those new boys. Joseph Absalom ordered somebody to go get 12 towels and 12 trash bags. With those supplies in hand, the new boys were marched around behind the armory, where they were instructed to remove their shoes, socks, and trousers, and put them in their trash bags, wrap the towels around themselves and go to their rooms to clean up. They were advised that they could go to the mess hall when they were done and their dinner would be saved for them. Our foolishness resulted in a lot of laughter that evening and the next day.

At lunch formation on Monday, Bones Gifford reached into his pocket, pulled out a card, then read it out loud, "Corporals Kowalski, Bass, Crawford and Brennan will report to Major Harden's office at 1600 hours sharp today." Gifford had a sheepish grin on his face.

Those nerds we thought, we'll fix them.

After mess Artie Mann approached Crawfish and me. "Sir, uh Sirs," he said, "None of us ratted on you guys, I swear, cross my heart and hope to die, we did not."

"How can you speak for all 12 of you?" asked Crawfish.

"We sit together at mess, and each of us swears that he didn't tell."

"So who did you tell, that might have told."

"Nobody, I swear, nobody."

"Artie Mann, you need to find out who ratted, or we will take it out on the 12 of you, as promised, do you understand?

"Yes sir, I'll try."

"Don't just try, do it!"

None of us were sure what punishment Hard-ass was going to give us, but we took one precaution. Each of us put on about 15 pair of jockey shorts. Between the first and second pair of mine, I stuffed a thin piece of sponge rubber over my butt.

We walked into Harden's office at 1600 hours sharp, "Corporals Bass, Brennan, Kowalski, and Crawford reporting as ordered, sir," I said.

As we stood at attention facing his desk, Major Harden asked, "Well, which one of you wants to tell me precisely what happened yesterday afternoon with the horse excreta?"

We had already predetermined that I would speak for the group as much as possible. Also, we knew from experience not to lie to Major Harden, because it would only make it tougher on us in the long run. We would try to tone it down as best we could. I started in, "Sir, it has always been a custom here at Kane Military Academy to sort of initiate the new boys. Last year when I was a new boy, I went through some things that were much worse than this horse manure thing, and I know for a fact that Corporals Kowalski, Crawford and Brennan experienced some terrible things too. Here it is late October, and we have not done anything until now to any of the new boys, and this was very mild, sir. We didn't hurt them in any way, except maybe their pride a little. Sir, everybody is always so serious here at school, so we thought a little prank might instill a little laughter and humor into the cadets. You know sir, horse manure is used to fertilize, cultivate, and enrich land to aid in the process of growing vegetables. Farmers handle it every day, and...

Harden interrupted, "Corporal Bass, I don't need a manure story. You boys were wrong to do what you did. You know that the administration here at Kane Military Academy frowns heavily on the hazing of new students. They tell their parents and other people and it conveys a poor impression of the school on whoever hears the story. All four of you were in trouble off and on last year. I would have thought you might have learned a few lessons by now. Where did the horse excreta come from anyway?"

"We have no idea, sir. I requested that they fetch some and they did. I assume that it probably came from one of the many ranches south of here, sir." Our eyes kept flashing over to the paddle that Hard-ass had hanging on his wall. The four of us had felt its sting several times last year. It was long and thin with large holes drilled through it, and it was nicely waxed. Attached to the handle was a small piece of rawhide in order to hang it from the wall.

"I am not going to bust your rank, nor am I going to paddle you, and you need not apologize to the new boys. But you are confined to the campus this coming weekend and will partake of Bull Ring Saturday morning, Saturday afternoon, and Sunday morning. Once you have completed those sessions of Bull Ring you will report back to me, at let's say 1400 hours Sunday. Do any of you have anything to say?"

"Sir, Corporal Brennan and I have prearranged dates with two girls from Hobart this weekend, and I am supposed to take delivery on my new car. Can we postpone this until the following weekend, sir?"

"No sir! Your car and your dates will just have to wait. That's an order!"

"Yes sir!"

"Dismissed!"

Damn, damn, damn, I thought. Linda is going to be pissed. She arranged a hot date for Squid so he could lose his virginity. Furthermore, it will be nearly three weeks that I haven't seen Linda by the time the following weekend rolls around. And, my new car, damn it, my new car. I won't even be able to see my new car for another whole week, actually almost two weeks from now. Damn, damn, damn. The only good thing about all of this, is that we missed half of our drill period because of our meeting with Major Harden.

CHAPTER TEN

Bull Ring

Every day during 4th period I watched Miss Mary Ann very carefully. She continued to wear tight sweaters and skirts above her knees. Even Tina didn't wear her skirts as short as Miss Mary Ann. Sometimes she would look directly at me, seeing that I was looking directly at her. Our eyes would catch momentarily, and then she would look away. I often wondered what she was thinking when she looked my way. I'll probably never know, I thought. Miss Mary Ann's auburn hair was in a bouffant. She was about as fine a specimen of a female as I had ever seen.

This week, time passed the slowest that I can remember. I wished that Bull Ring was behind us but it wasn't. I had to stand in line at the phones with my nickels in hand. It was imperative that I get through to Linda, Rooney, and Mom to let them know the change of plans. I spoke with Mom first, then Rooney, but had a heck of a time getting through to Linda. Finally, I did. "Hi Darling, I've got bad news." I thought she might be pissed. "Squid and I have been confined to the campus for the weekend, and have Bull Ring both Saturday and Sunday."

Linda chuckled, and said, "So, what's new? Think how many times you had it last year. What did you do this time?"

"I thought you would be pissed."

"Well, I am disappointed, but I'll tell Wanda and we'll get together the following weekend."

"You are very understanding, and that's one of the reasons I am crazy about you," I said.

"Why are you restricted?"

"Oh, it was nothing really, we just made some new boys march through horse shit over and over," I said.

Linda said, "Oh, those poor guys." Basically, she took the news fairly well.

Squid, Crawfish, Zebra and I were not the only cadets sentenced to Bull Ring. We were joined by Wilhelm von Kreisler III, a new boy that everybody called Billy. He was scheduled to serve five weeks of Bull Ring for threatening another cadet with a knife. Billy's father was one of the rocket engineers that the U.S. brought over from Germany after World War II. He had worked with Wernher von Braun on the *Vergeltungswaffe Zwei*, better known as the V-2 rocket, the long-range liquid-fuel ballistic missile that was the pet project of Adolph Hitler. Billy's father, who was a single parent, was currently working with von Braun at the Marshall Space Flight Center in Huntsville, Alabama, on the Redstone rocket that was powered by an engine similar to the V-2. He had little time for Billy, so he enrolled him at Kane. Billy hated Kane. He felt like he was in prison. The assignment of Bull Ring certainly didn't help matters.

The five of us were instructed to wear bathing suits, sweat shirts and tennis shoes when we reported for Bull Ring Saturday morning, so we did. We were instructed to go to the riverbank of the St. Johns, and drag out all of the branches, logs and trash that we could reach, pull them up the bank, and pile them in one pile in an open area so they could be burned once they dried out. It was a nasty job. The St. Johns was one of the few rivers in the world that flowed north. Anything that floated up the river usually wound up along the bank somewhere, and KMA had a long stretch of river frontage. We pulled out branches, brassieres, wood planks, underpants, logs, and beer bottles. We were sure that all that stuff didn't float down the river. Some of it most certainly was tossed down from the top of the bank.

"I am going to disappear," said Billy.

"Does that mean you are going to become invisible?" asked Squid, who obviously had read too many comic books.

"No, I am going to pack up and leave school, and never come back. I hate this place."

"Billy, what has your father said about your leaving?" I asked.

"He knows I hate it here, and he won't do anything about it, so I am going to leave and not tell him."

"If you go A.W.O.L. and get caught, you will be on Bull Ring for a long time," said Squid.

"If I am caught, I will leave again. This prison doesn't have any bars. They can't chain me down. I have plenty of money for transportation, so I am going to disappear," claimed

Billy.

As we approached the boathouse we noticed Cadet Howard Hill lying on top of the old navy boat.

"What are you doing, Hill?" I asked.

"I love boats. When I die I want to be buried in a boat," he said.

"Okay, but that boat is off-limits. What are you doing?

"I love boats. When I die I want to be buried in a boat," he repeated.

"I'll pass that information on to your assassin," I said. We walked off and left him alone. "That fellow is weird," I told the others, "He acts like he's been smoking opium It was getting close to time for us to quit, when Zebra nearly stepped on a water moccasin. "Look out!" I hollered. He jumped back, and the moccasin slithered away. "Damn," I said, "you don't want to get bitten by one of them. That guy will kill you, or put you in the hospital, for sure. Usually they will coil when you're that close." We got out of there quickly.

Our dress code for Saturday afternoon's Bull Ring was jeans, sweat shirts, and tennis shoes. Our task was to spread top soil over part of the drill field and seed it with rye grass. It was much easier work than our morning session, thank goodness. I glanced over at the main drive into Hard-ass Circle. "Geez, I know that car." I took off running toward the drive. The car belonged to Peachy, a friend of Linda's. I guess Peachy spotted me and stopped. As I got closer to the car, I could see Linda on the right side. She rolled down her window, and extended her arms.

"I am filthy dirty," I said, "but give me a kiss." We embraced, and kissed.

"Oh, you are getting me dirty," complained Linda.

"Sorry. What are you doing here?" I asked.

"I missed you and just took a chance that we could find you working out here somewhere, and we did," she said.

"Hi Peachy! Thanks for bringing her over."

"Hi Dean! Glad to do it."

"You know doll, I have this detail, and I can't stop working," I said, "but you have made my weekend by showing up here."

"I know. We better go. I love you!"

"I love you too!" I dashed back across the field and grabbed my shovel. Linda sure can be finicky, I thought.

"Deano, you know so many girls around here," said Crawfish, "why don't you fix me up
sometime."

"Crawfish, believe it or not, I have already tried. But the girls all tell me that Crawfish is so ugly, they would rather go out with an orangutan." I ragged him. "Say, are you going to New Orleans for Thanksgiving break?"

"Yeah! I am planning on it. Mother always has Thanksgiving dinner catered, and it is fantastic."

"Look, while you are over there, pick up about 2,000 feet each of green and yellow streamers.

"Don't get the purple. Can you do that?" I asked.

"Why green and yellow, but not purple? They are all Mardi Gras colors," Crawfish asked.

"Green and gold are our school colors, so just get green and yellow."

"I'll do it!"

"Say Deano, speaking of Thanksgiving, why don't you ride down to Miami with me for the holiday?" asked Squid, "we'll go deep sea fishing."

"That sounds like fun," I said, "let me clear it with Linda."

"Damn Deano," Zebra chirped in, "you are getting henpecked. You can't do anything without your old lady's permission."

I just laughed. After we got cleaned up that evening, we went to mess. Mess was a mess. We were served hot dogs and sauerkraut. I hate hot dogs and sauerkraut. What kind of a meal is that for a Saturday evening dinner? Whenever we didn't like Willie's menu, we would show our displeasure by putting the little square butter patties on the ends of our knives and then snapping them up so they stuck on the ceiling. The butter might stick for as long as an hour on that stippled ceiling, and made it very difficult for Willie and his crew to clean up the mess hall. Willie eventually got wise and served the butter frozen. Frozen butter would hit the ceiling and come right back down. After mess we headed to the snack machines in order to supplement our meal, then on to the smoking lounge. We dropped some coins into the Wurlitzer juke box, and settled in for some serious 8-ball.

Sunday morning we lucked out. It was raining so they couldn't work us outside. We were escorted to the laundry room which was closed. It smelled like shit. I wondered if the odor could have lingered that long from the new boys' trousers and socks. After we spread copies of the Jacksonville newspapers across the floor we were given two gallons of baby-doo yellow paint and five 3-inch brushes. We actually did a fantastic job of painting that room, and were even commended afterward by Major Harden for doing such a superb job.

After we cleaned up, it was time for mess. We couldn't believe it. We were served turkey, dressing, mashed potatoes, peas and carrots, cranberry, rolls and apple cobbler. There was even enough for seconds. Absolutely no butter got slung up to the ceiling. We praised Willie for the fine meal. He said, "I can't always do this you know. I have a tight budget for groceries. It all depends on what the school gives me to spend." I guess he was making an excuse for meals like the hot dogs and sauerkraut that he served on Saturday evening.

After mess, Zebra, Crawfish, Squid and I adjourned to the smoking lounge where we spent the rest of the afternoon.

CHAPTER ELEVEN

Coors

Study periods were every evening from Sunday through Thursday, so Squid and I settled in at our two-sided desk Sunday evening and discussed a number of different subjects. "Why do you want Crawfish to get those green and yellow streamers?" Squid asked.

"Because, I am going to drape them all over Southside High School."

"Instead of the paint you talked about."

"Yep, at least we won't be destroying any property. We can get in there and out quickly, and won't get caught," I said.

"We could still get caught."

"If we are, big deal. They aren't going to charge us with dispensing streamers."

"It's better than the paint," said Squid. "Why don't we take our lime and lime cart over there and letter their field, like they did ours?"

"That would be risky. All those apartments behind the school overlook the end zone of the football field. Somebody would see us for sure, even at night."

"I still think we should consider it. When there's a will, there's a way," said Squid. "Hey, are we rescheduled next weekend with Linda and Wanda? Do you know Wanda? What does she look like?"

"Hell Squid, I think she weighs about 300 pounds, but she wants your bod."

"Seriously, is she fat?"

"I have no idea what she looks like, but Linda isn't going to fix you up with a dog, trust her. Everything should be a go, so plan to head home with me. Fact is, I have no wheels and need a ride anyway."

"When will you pick your car up?"

"Saturday," I said, and then changed the subject. "I am having some beer delivered. I wonder where it is."

"Do you put a rubber on before you get dressed or just

before you have sex?" asked Squid, who couldn't get his mind off getting laid.

"Just before."

"Just before what?"

"Just before you have intercourse," I said.

"You know, we forgot to get rubbers when we came back to school."

"We can stop at the Sinclair station up the street, they have a dispenser."

"Don't forget!"

"You're driving. You need them. You remember."

"Don't you use rubbers?"

"No!"

"How come?"

"Just don't."

"Where are we going to have sex?" asked Squid.

"I don't know, we'll play it by ear."

"How about the back seat of your new car? I'd like to break in your new car."

"No, besides we'll have your car Friday night."

"We always take my car. Did you know that Esso just announced an eight-tenths of one cent increase in their gas prices? And, gas is already 29 cents per gallon," said Squid.

"Big deal," I said, "that means it will cost us one penny more to go from here to the beach. Besides, I always chip in on your gas, don't I?"

"Yeah."

"Say, how do you think Crawfish got a key to Dames' old apartment?" I questioned, "He won't tell anyone how he came up with it,"

"I have no idea," indicated Squid.

"What do you think of the new chemistry teacher, Captain Bohanon?"

"You mean BoBo, he is a little strange. Have you seen his car? He must have 30 old 'I like Ike' decals plastered all over that Hudson," said Squid.

"He does seem a little gung-ho."

"I hope you can go to Miami with me for Thanksgiving."

"If I do, can we go to one of those joints that has the totally nude dancers?"

"I doubt if we could get in, Deano."

"What if we chalked our hair, and wore some old granny glasses."

"I still doubt that we could get in," repeated Squid. "I know one thing. I better take care of Granny's ashes before we go because Dad will raise hell with me if I haven't."

"Hell Squid, just bury the ashes on the riverbank. She'll be close enough to your Grandfather out there." I wasn't serious.

"You are heartless, Deano. Would you bury your grandmother on the riverbank?"

"Is it my imagination, or are Mary Ann's skirts getting shorter every week?" I changed the subject.

"Seems like it to me too."

"Maybe she hems them up about a half-inch higher each week, just to tease us."

"I wouldn't be surprised," said Squid. "Say, do you think there is a chance we will get drafted into military service after we graduate?"

"That is probably a very slim possibility," I said. "Things have cooled off in Korea, and they aren't taking college students. So, unless a new war breaks out, you shouldn't have to worry about it. But, if they draft us, they draft us, and we will get to see the world. We can also get some of our college education out of the way while we're in the service."

There was a tap on the open door and we looked up to see Joey Tighe, a day student, standing in the doorway. "I got your six-pack Deano, but I couldn't bring it through the main entrance. Here are your S&H green stamps."

"Thanks Joey, I will drop a line down from the side window here. Tie it around the handle part of the six-pack, so the bottles don't fall out, and I'll hoist it up to the room. Did I give you enough money to cover the cost?"

"Yes," he responded, "is it safe to hoist that beer up here?"

"Sure, just tie the line well." I dropped the line from the side window. Joey went down, fetched the beer from his car and tied it to the line I had dropped. I hoisted it up to our third floor room. "All right! Look at this Squid, its Coors. Where did Joey get this, I wonder, and it's nice and cold too." In 1955 Coors did not market their products in the eastern states. They felt that their "Made with Rocky Mountain Spring Water" slogan wouldn't sell in the east. The only way you could get Coors was from somebody that "imported" a supply from Mexico or from the western states. There was another tap on the open door. This time it was that weirdo, Howard Hill, who roomed in the tower room on the second floor, just below us.

"Hey you guys, I was sitting at my desk and saw a six-pack ascend past my window. So, I sneaked up the tower stairs to get my share."

"Your share is one bottle, Hill. Take it and get out of here before you get us all in trouble." I knew if I gave him one, he wouldn't rat. It was better than taking a chance. A few minutes later, Hill's roommate, Dwight, was standing at our door. I had to give him a beer also, but at least that left two each for me and Squid.

"What are you men up to?" snapped a voice from our doorway. It was Joseph Absalom, the cadet battalion commander.

"What do you mean, sir? I asked."

"You know very well what I mean. How many do you have left."

"Four sir," I figured I better not lie. He must have seen Hill or his roommate walking out with a beer.

"Hand them over! I am confiscating them." indicated Absalom, and he walked out the door with our beer and a grin on his face. We knew that Absalom loved beer, and we were fairly certain that he split them with his roommate.

I folded my arms on my desk, and rested my head on my arms. "This has not been a good weekend," I moaned.

"You are right about that," added Squid.

Monday morning rolled around, and there was no sign of Wilhelm von Kreisler III. As he had indicated he would do, he had disappeared. Major Harden addressed us during breakfast mess formation.

"Anybody that knows anything about the absence of Cadet Wilhelm von Kreisler, please fall out and report to my office. You will not miss breakfast."

Billy's roommate Carl, Squid, Zebra, Crawfish, and I all fell out. Those of us who were on Bull Ring with Billy, explained to Hard-ass what he had said about disappearing. Carl added quite a bit more. He indicated that he thought Billy was going to commit suicide by shooting himself or drowning himself.

"Billy didn't take very many things with him. I know he had a lot of money, but if he was going to travel very far I would have thought he might have taken more clothes and other belongings with him," said Carl. "I know he was really down in the dumps. If I had to guess, I believe he will kill himself."

That was all Major Harden needed to hear. He picked up the telephone and called the police. He reported Billy as a missing person, and was preparing to call Billy's father when he dismissed us. After breakfast we noticed two police cars parked on Hard-ass Circle, so they must have responded quickly.

My thoughts were with Billy. I hoped he would be okay. He was really a cool guy, even if he was a new boy.

CHAPTER TWELVE

Granny's Ashes

Carrie and I were excused from our respective schools on Tuesday at the request of my father. Horace Bacon, Dad's vice-president at the shipyard, died the previous Friday as a result of a massive heart attack. It was important to Dad for our entire family to attend the funeral to show our respect for his right hand man.

Mom and Dad were viewing the casket during the late morning while Carrie and I were killing time wandering about the funeral home. I noticed a display of urns and boxes used to preserve the ashes of the dead after cremation. There it was, a burgundy box with a gold cross affixed to the lid, identical to the one sitting on Squid's dresser that contained his grandmother's ashes. I purchased it immediately, had it put in a bag, and carried it out to Dad's Pontiac. Later, after we returned home from the cemetery, I took the box into the house and filled it with ashes from our living room fireplace. I put the box back into the bag and took it back to school that evening. I was still without wheels, so Mom picked me up, and also returned me to Kane Military. That was great because I got to drive her Cadillac from school and then again on the return trip.

After taps that night, I lay on my bunk until I was certain that Squid was asleep. Once I was sure that he was, I eased from my bunk. There was just enough light from the hall coming through the hole where the door knob used to be for me to see. I removed the box containing Granny's ashes from the top of Squid's dresser. I placed it in a good hiding place, under some thermal underwear in his bottom drawer. I took the identical box, containing the fireplace ashes, and put it on top of Squid's dresser in the exact spot where Granny had been. After doing so, I quietly eased back into my bunk and went to sleep.

A prank is much more effective when you share it with others. After breakfast, I cornered Zebra, Brad and Crawfish and let them in on my scheme. After our last period, we will all meet in my room. With Squid present, I will accidently drop the burgundy box on the floor. The lid will pop off and the ashes will scatter all over the floor. Squid will be distraught. Attempting to help, Crawfish will then step on the ashes dispersing them even more. He will step away tracking the ashes across the room. I will apologize vehemently for disseminating Granny all over the room. Squid will freak out. The guys loved the plan and confirmed that they would be there after last period.

I was slightly detained after my last class, and Squid, Zebra, Brad and Crawfish were all in the room ahead of me. I glanced at the top of Squid's dresser and there was no burgundy box. Could they be playing a trick on me, I wondered. No, they wouldn't have had time to even discuss it, I thought. "Where is Granny?" I asked.

Major Harden drove Granny and me over to Thorncrown Cemetery during my free period this morning. I had Granny sealed in her niche forever," said Squid. "The folks over there are very nice. Within the next few weeks they will have a name plate inscribed that they will affix to Granny's niche."

Oh my God, I thought. The fireplace ashes are in the niche while Granny remains beneath the thermal underwear. "I am going to the smoking lounge," I said, and then departed. Brad, Zebra and Crawfish sensing the seriousness of the calamity followed me downstairs.

"Damn Deano, what are you going to do?" asked Brad.

"I have no idea, but I have to do something to get the real Granny into her niche, and I need to do it without Squid finding out."

"Maybe you should just tell Squid what happened and let him get the boxes swapped out," suggested Crawfish.

"Not a chance! I created the problem, and I need to get it resolved. I don't want Squid to know what happened. I am going to make a phone call and then I'll see you guys in the smoking lounge."

I placed a call to Thorncrown Cemetery to find out if a niche could be opened. The lady I spoke with informed me that once a niche is sealed it takes a court order to have it opened back up.

I told Brad, Crawfish and Zebra what the lady said.

"Hell, you could break into the niche and swap out the

boxes," claimed Brad.

"I don't even know what niche it is. I won't know until they put the inscription on it. Furthermore, that would be like opening a grave. They would put me under the jail for that, if I got caught. Think y'all! There has to be some solution to this problem."

"What if the real Granny's ashes reappeared on top of Squid's dresser? It would drive him batty trying to figure out what happened. He would probably have the niche reopened just to confirm that the box was or wasn't there," said Brad. "The trick would be in convincing him somehow that the box that reappeared was the real Granny."

"If he had the niche opened maybe we could convince him to put both boxes inside. That way he should know that his Granny was in one or the other. At least he would have the peace of mind of knowing that she was in the niche," said Crawfish.

"He would be wondering about it for the rest of his life," I said. "The real Granny needs to replace the fireplace ashes somehow without Squid ever knowing about it." The thought crossed my mind that I had better get Granny out from under the thermal underwear and put her somewhere safe. I wouldn't want her to turn up during an inspection. That would really blow Squid's mind. I had just about made my mind up that I needed to open that niche somehow, and trade boxes.

Once again I waited for Squid to fall asleep before I quietly climbed from my bunk. I slowly opened Squid's bottom drawer, reached in and removed the burgundy box with the gold cross on top. Suddenly, Squid jumped down from the top bunk and flipped on the light. He caught me red-handed holding Granny's ashes. "What's going on?" he asked. I had no choice but to tell him the whole story of my plan for a prank, how I bought an identical box, how I was going to dump the fireplace ashes all over the floor, and how the plan totally backfired. Squid said, "Hell it is no problem. As far as anybody is concerned Granny is in that niche." He reached for the box and I gave it to him. He opened the lid, walked into the bathroom and proceeded to dump the ashes down the commode, laughing the whole time he did it. "Well, there goes Granny down the drain." Squid continued to laugh. I just sat there not believing what I was seeing. He laughed so hard he was almost hysterical. Thank goodness we were isolated down in the tower room or he would have awakened everyone on the hall.

"I'm sorry Squid. When I saw that identical box at the funeral parlor it had trick written all over it. I couldn't resist." Squid continued to laugh. I couldn't believe he flushed his grandmother away into the sewer line.

"Deano, I must confess. I am a light sleeper. When you originally opened my bottom drawer and placed something in there, I saw you, and knew you were up to something. In the morning, while you were in the shower, I checked things out. What you didn't know was that the box that contained Granny's ashes had a small inscription on the bottom of it. So, it was easy for me to see that you were up to something. This morning Major Harden drove me to Thorncrown with the box that actually had Granny's ashes. She is now safe in her niche. The ashes that I just flushed down the commode were the ones from your fireplace at home.

"Squid, I will never play another prank on you. I should say, I will never attempt to play another prank on you. The best laid plans of mice and men sometimes go astray."

CHAPTER THIRTEEN

What's A Bikini?

We checked out Friday afternoon, and were glad to get away from Kane. A few miles down the road, I said, "Damn Squid, we forgot to stop at the Sinclair station and get condoms. Pull into that Atlantic-Richfield station and let's check the men's room." He stopped, and we both headed toward the rest room.

"Damn Squid, listen to that. Somebody's in there upchucking. That is so nasty."

"I'll check the colored men's restroom. The door's open."

"Yeah, there should be machines in there also. Colored folks do the do too."

As we stood in the colored men's room scrutinizing the three dispensers on the wall, Squid said, "Hey Deano, what's a French tickler?"

I explained it to him. "Just get a couple of those plain ones, they'll do the trick."

We had been at the house less than an hour when Linda called. "I have some bad news," she said.

"What?"

"Wanda just got her period and isn't feeling well. She said she is not making love while she is on her period - period!"

"That's a bummer."

"It is too late to get Squid another date tonight. Being that he is there, why don't you guys do something tonight, and I will try to line him up with somebody else tomorrow night. Is that alright with you?"

"Well sure, I'll pass the word on to Squid. Let's touch base early tomorrow afternoon." Linda and I talked for another 15 minutes or so before we hung up.

When I told Squid about Wanda, he just looked at me with a blank stare. "I guess I'll be a virgin the rest of my life," he said.

"Don't get down in the dumps. Look at the bright side. Linda will probably fix you up tomorrow night, and I have some good news. She said her Aunt Jan's family was going to be visiting them for a few days over Thanksgiving, so it is fine with her if I go to Miami with you."

"Great!"

"But I still think we should try to get into one of those nudie places."

"Well, I'm not against trying. The worst thing that could happen is that they say no."

"I agree."

Squid took his suitcase up to his room. As I headed down the hall toward the kitchen, Tina was coming the other way. She gave me a wink, and then a hug. Damn, I thought, she had never done that before. Was she trying to tell me something?

I called Rooney and advised him that I would pick my car up late morning tomorrow. Susan prepared a really good meal that evening, pot roast with veggies. I love pot roast with veggies. Squid and I ate so much that after dinner we adjourned to the den and flopped into easy chairs to watch the Green Hornet on one of our four television channels. Carrie joined us after a while. I couldn't believe she didn't have a date. She almost always was going somewhere. The thought crossed my mind that we could take Carrie, and pick up Linda, and then go to a movie. Then I thought better of it, and it was starting to get late. "I heard you guys had Bull Ring last weekend," she said.

"Yes, and it was pitiful," said Squid. He talked to Carrie every chance he had.

"Is Dean getting you into trouble again? He is so bad."

"You are just as bad, Carrie. I don't want to hear another word," I said.

"Don't pick on Carrie," said Squid, "she's a cool girl."

"Thank you Squid," she said, smiling at him.

"Carrie is my sister, and I'll pick on her any time I want to," I said as I grinned at her in jest. With that, we changed the subject.

The folks were in the living room, watching our other television. We were the only family I knew of that had two televisions. Mom loved Tommy and Jimmy Dorsey, and also the Lawrence Welk Show. It looked like they were watching one of them when I popped my head in to let her know that I would be gone over the Thanksgiving holiday.

Needless to say, Squid and I didn't go anywhere that evening. I finally retired to my room about 10:30 p.m. leaving Squid and Carrie engrossed in a game of gin rummy.

I showered and dressed Saturday morning and left my room. All of the doors on the second floor were still closed, so I knew everybody was sleeping in. When I got down to the kitchen, there was Tina wrapped in a bathrobe, pouring herself a glass of orange juice.

We said our good mornings, and then I added, "Ever since you have been working here you have never winked at me or hugged me until yesterday, why now?"

She grinned and said, "maybe I never felt like it until yesterday," and she winked again.

"Well, you can hug me anytime you want," I said, "It felt good when you pressed your body against mine." I was getting brave.

"Dean, you must be horny."

"Nope, I get laid plenty. I am not the least bit horny." As the conversation progressed, Tina got a lot more personal.

"I bought several new bikini panties from a mail order place called Frederick's of Hollywood. I sent them a check, and two weeks later my bikinis arrived.

"What's a bikini?" I asked.

"You've never heard of a bikini?"

"Nope!"

"I guess you've never seen one either then."

"Nope!"

"They are low cut and sexy," she said as she took my hand and dragged me into her room. She closed her door behind us. If I show you one, you must promise not to ever tell a single soul that I did."

I promised, thinking that she would pull one out of a drawer and show me. But she certainly took me by surprise. Tina undid the tie on her robe belt, opened her robe, and let it fall to the floor. Except for her very shear, and I mean see through, skimpy panties, she was wearing nothing. Her tits looked fantastic, with their pink nipples. And, those panties, lord, I could see every pubic hair she had through them. "So that's a bikini, huh?" I said, as I stooped down to get a closer look. As my eyes were about at bikini level, she put her hand behind my head and pulled my face against her body. My heart was definitely racing as I stood up. "Tina, you are the horny one."

"I'm not horny Dean Bass, I just want you," she said. "I want to have sex with you right now."

"Okay, we'll do it, but not now. I hear voices out in the kitchen."

"Then when?"

"I don't know, but we'll find an appropriate time."

"Promise," she asked.

"I promise."

She put her arms around me and gave me the wettest, sloppiest kiss ever. I just couldn't resist doing what I did next. I bent over and wrapped my lips around her left nipple momentarily, then scooted out her outside entrance. I just couldn't resist putting that nipple in my mouth, just absolutely couldn't resist. As I walked around the house to let myself in the front door, I thought, wow, what have I committed myself to?

A couple of hours later, Squid took me to Rooney's. My car was beautiful. It was painted black with a few yellow, orange, and red flames leaping out of the front wheel wells, and a little very tasteful accent striping around the windows, skirts, and elsewhere. The interior was also redone. Rooney repeated what the people at Marlin Chrysler-Plymouth had told me. "Drive it easy for a couple of weeks until it's broken in." I could feel its power even though I didn't open it up. Squid loved the car, and immediately named it "Fireball." It was a far cry from my old turdmobile.

When we got back to the house, Dad walked out to see the car. "That's not the car I bought," he said, "the contract says it's two-tone, white and black."

"Sir, it is now four-tone, I had it repainted with my own money." said I.

"Well, it's different," said Dad, "I feel sure there is not another like it in the world. When you're home please park it in the garage so nobody can see it." I think he was just being sarcastic. I knew that wasn't going to happen. We had a three car garage. Dad's Kaiser Darrin was his pride and joy so it took preference.

Mom's Cadillac convertible had its own special spot. Dad's Pontiac Star Chief Catalina, his work car, was brand new so he surely was going to always use the third stall. Carrie was getting a car soon, and our employees Tina and Susan each had their own cars, so our circular drive looked like a parking lot most of the time.

Sharon was at the house, so she and Carrie had to go for a spin. Squid jumped in the back seat with Carrie, and Sharon up front with me. I remembered what Carrie told me that Sharon had said. She sure was pretty, naked or clothed. I not only had my mind on Sharon, but I kept picturing Tina standing there in her new shear bikini panties. We drove around so long that I almost forgot to call Linda. When we arrived back at the house, I dashed in and called her.

"Squid has a date with Peachy tonight," Linda said, "He'll enjoy her company, but remember, she's a goody-goody so there won't be any sex. Okay?"

"Sure, he's handled it this long, a little longer won't hurt."

"We'd sure like to go see *The Seven Year Itch* with Marilyn Monroe. Would y'all mind taking us to see it?"

"Heck no, I just want to be with you. I'll take you any-where," I said.

Squid had met Peachy before and of course vice-versa. He was happy just to have a date, so there were no complaints from him. He did ask several questions, however, "How long do rubbers last? Where should I keep them? What if the officers' find them during inspection? Do I need to keep them in a refrigerator? Can I get my money back at the gas station, if I don't use them?"

"Keep them in your car, but don't open them. If you open them the lubrication will dry out," I said. "We aren't having much luck. You probably will be a virgin the rest of your life."

Squid didn't think that was the least bit funny.

The girls loved my car. At least they said they did. We drove around some before we went to the theater. "Linda, some of the guys and their girlfriends are planning a 'jungle party.' Everybody is supposed to dress like Tarzan and Jane. I thought it might be a cool get-together. Should we go?" I asked. "You're welcome to go too, Peachy."

"Forget about it," Linda responded. "You will never catch

me dressed in a leopard skin looking outfit. I'll leave that for the hookers down on Bay Street."

"Oh well, pretend I never mentioned it." Linda sure was stuffy about a lot of things. She just didn't know how to really have fun, I thought.

After the movie we went to eat some big, juicy 19-cent hamburgers at a new restaurant called the Burger King. While we were sitting there pigging out on our food, I couldn't resist bringing up "bikinis."

"Have either of you girls bought any of those new bikini panties?" I asked.

"I haven't," claimed Peachy.

"How do you know about bikini panties?" asked Linda.

"Oh, I saw them in a magazine. They look sexy."

"I bought some," said Linda, "from a mail order place called Frederick's of Hollywood. In fact, I was wearing one the last time we went to the beach, but I guess it was too dark for you to notice."

I was glad to see that Linda was in sync with the fashion world. Well, she wasn't stuffy about everything, thank goodness.

"Hey Peachy, are you a virgin?" I asked jokingly.

"That's none of your business, Mr. Bass," she quipped.

I hadn't told Squid about Tina, and didn't plan to.

"What's a bikini?" he asked.

CHAPTER FOURTEEN

The Fair

Sunday morning, Carrie, Squid, and I went horseback riding at the Starwood Stables. There were some neat and lengthy trails that led from the stables, so you could ride out, do a large loop and come back from a different direction. Carrie and I both had several friends that frequented Starwood.

After we dropped Carrie back at the house, about 2 p.m. we took off in both cars for school. My new car got a ton of attention at school. Actually, I worried about it sitting in the parking lot, with those crazies from Southside High wandering around.

There was one weekend left before the Thanksgiving holiday, so I checked out, by myself, so I could spend as much time with Linda as possible. The fair was in town at the Lenox Avenue fairgrounds, so Linda and I decided to go on Saturday. The midway was awesome, and there were plenty of booths where you could win stuffed animals. It was something that I was pretty good at.

At one end of the midway there were several tents that had freaky stuff in them. For a fee you could enter a tent and view a two-headed calf. Another had the world's smallest man. We never knew whether he was alive, or a corpse, because we didn't go in there to see. In an adjacent tent was a corpse of what they called a morphodite, a body that was half woman, half man. We didn't go into that tent either.

We never knew his real name, but we called him "Train Man," because the feeble minded soul spent much of each day running up and down the railroad tracks around Jacksonville. He carried a board with a leather strap attached to it over his shoulder as he ran. Nobody had any idea what the significance of that board was, but he always had it as he ran. Most everybody knew about Train Man, and he was actually the object of many jokes. Well, here he was at the fair, just walking around, without his board, seemingly enjoying the fanfare. The midway had a ride called the "Comet." It went around in circles at a high rate of speed, and tilted up as it went, to an almost vertical position. I asked Train Man if he would like to ride the Comet, and he indicated that he would. So, I bought him a ticket, and he climbed into one of the cars. He had a big smile on his face as the Comet started up, and gained speed. The smile turned to a frown as the ride tilted upwards. I told Linda that maybe this wasn't such a good idea. Train Man's face turned to a grief stricken look, and suddenly Linda and I were splattered with spots of blood. Each time the Comet revolved we were hit by more spots of blood. I hollered at the ride operator to shut it down. He didn't hear me at first, but then he slowed the ride, eventually bringing it to a stop. The blood was coming from Train Man's nose. I apologized to Train Man as we escorted him to the emergency medical trailer for first aid care.

One of the tents had milk cans bunched in the center of the booth. Anyone that could toss a softball into the mouth of a milk can would win his or her choice of large stuffed animals. The openings were a fraction of an inch larger than the diameter of the softball. And, the softballs were not soft, but hard, so they would readily bounce away when they hit the rim of the milk can.

Three tosses for 50 cents and one in would win your choice. I gave the attendant 50 cents, and quickly tossed one of the balls into one of the cans. I chose a giant teddy bear, and the attendant passed it across the counter to me. As he was doing so, I felt a tug on my trouser leg. I looked down and a little girl was standing there holding a half-dollar. She looked pitiful, in tattered clothes, with messed up hair, and bare feet. Her mother, who looked just as pitiful, was standing off a distance away.

"Sir," the little girl said, as she tried to hand me the half-dollar piece. "Would you win me a stuffed animal too?"

Well, I wasn't going to take her half-dollar, nor was I very sure that I could just toss another ball into another milk can. She looked so pathetic standing there thinking that I could win a stuffed animal for her, that my compassion took over.

"Here angel," I said. "You keep your half-dollar, and take this teddy bear home with you. I hope you get a lot of enjoyment from it."

"Oh, thank you very much, sir," she said with a huge smile on her face. Her mother thanked me also.

"That was so sweet of you," said Linda.

"Well, now I have to win another one, because that was yours that I just gave away."

It took $8.00 to win another teddy bear. I probably could have bought four teddy bears at a toy store for that 8 dollars. But, Linda had a stuffed animal, and the little girl and her mother were happy.

"Do you think the little girl's mother put her up to that?" I asked Linda.

"Of course she did. The girl wouldn't have had a half-dollar in her hand if her mother hadn't given it to her."

As we walked toward the roller coaster, appropriately named "Sudden Fear," I suggested to Linda, "Hey, let's ride it!"

"Not me. Those things scare me to death." she confessed.

"Hey, do you see those girls getting off the coaster? The blond is Sharon, Carrie's best friend, and the redhead is Tricia. They are both cheerleaders." Sharon spotted me as they exited through the coaster's gate.

"Dean!" she called out, and we headed toward each other. Sharon did something she had never done the whole time I have known her. She put her arms around my neck and gave me a soft little kiss. I couldn't help but grin. "It's good to see you, she said."

"Hi Sharon! Hi Tricia!" I said, and then introduced them both to Linda.

"I sure like your new car, Dean," said Sharon. "It is so fast."

Sharon has a little devilish streak in her. She would never have kissed me if Linda had not been there. She just wanted to cause a little friction, and did a good job of it.

The four of us talked for several minutes, and then Linda and I split.

"That girl is gorgeous." Linda said, and then added, "You looked like you enjoyed that kiss. I saw that big grin on your face. When did she ride in your new car?"

"Don't make something out of nothing. She is Carrie's friend, so she is over at our house quite often."

"How often does she kiss you like that?"

"That was the first time." I said, but I could tell Linda didn't believe me as she rolled her eyes. "Do I detect a little jealousy?" I asked.

"No! Just forget it." she said.

We spent part of Saturday evening parked on the bank of the Ortega River, making love.

Linda went to church Sunday morning, and then she drove over to my house for dinner.

I told Linda goodbye late Sunday afternoon, then went upstairs to pack for our Miami trip. Squid and I could check out after class on Wednesday, and didn't have to be back until class Tuesday morning, so we decided to leave directly from school and head south. We also decided to take Fireball, and leave Squid's car at Kane. As I was pulling things out of drawers, Tina walked in. She threw her arms around me and gave me another wet, sloppy kiss, and then she said, "Everybody just left, the house is empty. It's a good time."

"No, no, no, I am in a rush to get packed and back to school. It will have to wait until another time."

"Please."

"Listen, I want you too." I said, as I reached out and felt her boobs, "but I just don't have time now."

"All right, just remember you promised," she said, and stayed in the room helping me pack. One more wet kiss and I was out of there. Damn, I thought, I'll bet she really is good in bed.

I gassed up at a Gulf station, collected my S&H Green Stamps, and drove back to school. My thoughts jumped back and forth from Linda to Tina to Sharon to Miss Mary Ann. I think I lusted for them all.

As classes let out on Wednesday I ran into Miss Mary Ann in the corridor. "Don't you have a car on campus, Corporal Bass?"

"Yes ma'am."

"I was wondering if I could impose upon you to stop by my apartment sometime over the
holiday, and help me move some furniture."

"I would be glad to do it, but I am driving Corporal Brennan down to Miami, and won't be back until classes begin next Tuesday. Can the furniture moving wait until after I get back?"

She looked me right in the eye, and said, "I can wait, if you'll promise to help me."

"I promise."

Miss Mary Ann reached into the purse she was carrying and handed me a piece of paper. I stuck it in my pocket without reading it. "Okay," she said, "I'm going to hold you to that promise."

As soon as I got out of her sight I opened the paper. It contained her address, apartment number, and telephone number all neatly printed. Holy shit, I thought, she preplanned this. She already had the note written, and arranged to bump into me in the corridor. And, another promise. What is this with all these promises? I dashed up the stairs to our room and told Squid what happened.

"I told you, she wants your bod," he said.

"I don't know man, she may just want me to help her move some furniture."

"Bull shit Deano, she wants you. When are you going over there?"

"I have no idea. I guess when we get back."

"You are one lucky son-of-a-bitch," Squid said.

"Don't tell a soul about this, okay?"

"Yeah, yeah, okay!"

"I mean really, don't mention it to anybody."

CHAPTER FIFTEEN

The Vagabonds

We loaded my car and pointed it south. Miami or bust. When we got to Ormond Beach, we saw a sign that said, "All the seafood you can eat for $1.25." I hit the brakes and we indulged. I mean we indulged. We ate, and we ate, and we ate some more. The manager walked over to our table.

"Where are you boys from?" he asked.

"Jacksonville," I said.

"Do you come through here very often?"

"Not very often."

"How would you boys like to eat free next time you come through here?"

"That would be nice."

"Well," he said, stop in here and I'll give you each $1.25 so you can go across the street to see my competitor. He also has an 'all you can eat' deal for $1.25."

Once we were back in the car, I said, "was he serious?"

"I guess so. We must have eaten all his profit up."

As we passed Daytona Beach, I said, "Squid, we should come down here for the Grand National Stock Car Race in February. It's a 160 mile race, half on the beach, half on Atlantic Avenue. There are a zillion cars in it, and lots of wrecks. I think it is a 4.1 mile oval, but I can't remember for sure."

"Have you been before?"

"Yeah, it is quite a spectacle. The start-finish line is on Atlantic Avenue. When the cars come down the beach heading toward the 3rd turn, where they go up a ramp, they start gearing down, and sliding. By the time the race is over they will have dug a huge hole in the sand. Lets plan to go, it will be on a Sunday, I think."

"Sounds good to me," said Squid.

As we rolled down U.S. 1, through the state of Florida, most of our discussion centered around women, and one in particular, Miss Mary Ann.

"You know Deano, if you were to bounce on the springs

with her, you might be getting it on with the most beautiful woman in the city."

"I know, but I'm not sure she is better looking than Carrie's friend Sharon."

"Miss Mary Ann is more beautiful than Marilyn Monroe, or Jayne Mansfield, or, Lana Turner, or Elizabeth Taylor, or..."

"I know," I repeated.

"If you did make love to her, would you use a rubber?"

"Not unless she wanted me to."

"Those tight sweaters she wears don't leave much to the imagination"

"I know."

"You know Deano, I could play with one of her boobs, and you could play with the other at the same time, and we would never get in each others way."

"I know."

"Do you really think she raises her hemline a little each week?"

"Sure seems like it. Her skirts just keep getting shorter."

"Why do you think Kane would hire such a gorgeous chick?"

"Probably to torture us."

"Maybe Hard-ass is tired of looking at Mrs. Hard-ass, and wanted a looker to churn his butter. Know what I mean?"

"Maybe."

"Why would she want to work at a boys school?"

"Probably so she could tease us."

"She damn sure teases me," said Squid.

"Me too."

There was a Western Auto store still open in Cocoa so we stopped. I bought a new doggie knob for my steering wheel, and borrowed a screwdriver to put it on.

It was getting late when we finally arrived in Miami. This was actually my second trip to Squid's house. He had driven me down for a long holiday weekend last year, so I had met his parents, and had gone deep sea fishing with him before. Thursday was Thanksgiving, and Mrs. Brennan prepared a marvelous dinner, with turkey and all the trimmings. We stuffed ourselves, I called Linda to wish her a happy Thanksgiving, and then we took off for downtown Miami to see what kind of action we could find. Mr. Brennan had one of his charters scheduled for us at 8 a.m., so we didn't want to stay out too late. His boats were booked up Saturday and Sunday, so Friday was the only day he could oblige us with a private charter.

On Biscayne Blvd. there was a place called the Vagabonds. After parking, we mixed in with a few old men and were able to walk right in, with no questions asked. We sat next to the old-timers, so it looked like we were part of their group. The burlesque show had some fairly decent looking strippers alternating with a corny comedian and an average juggler. Our seats were right at the edge of the stage, so the dancers flaunted their bodies just a few feet from Squid's bulging eyeballs. We tucked one dollar bills into each stripper's g-string, until the stripper removed her g-string and there wasn't any place left to tuck. When they weren't on the stage, the girls circulated getting patrons to buy them drinks. They would order gin cocktails at the exorbitant price of $1.25 each, but were simply served 7-Up by the bartender. Naturally, the management wanted their strippers to remain sober. It was all a game to fleece their customers of as many greenbacks as they could. We played along a little bit, and had fun. Squid couldn't hold his liquor very well and was totally inebriated by about midnight. We thought about leaving and going elsewhere, but we weren't sure we could get in anywhere else, so we just stayed at the Vagabonds.

The clubs in Miami stayed open all night, and we were enjoying ourselves so much that we completely lost track of time. Eventually, I looked at my Omega. 5 a.m. it said. "Damn, we have to be on that charter in three hours. C'mon Squid, let's get out of here!" I said.

By the time we stopped at Wolfie's Restaurant for breakfast, and picked up a supply of beer for the boat, and went to Squid's house to change, and drove over to Pier 5, it was time to board our boat. I had a fake ID, so it was never a problem buying beer. As we walked down the dock toward the *Lady Mae*, the captain and mate spotted us and just shook their heads in disbelief. We did not look good. Nor, did we feel real good. The ocean was a little rough, but Squid and I had both been on plenty of boats, so we didn't get sick. We headed out to the Gulf Stream, about eleven miles from shore, where the best fishing is located. Oscar was our captain, and Sky our mate. Sky took care of all the bait, so we didn't even get our hands messy. Squid attempted to climb the ladder to the bridge. He ascended about three or four rungs before he fell back unhurt onto the rear deck. At that point he climbed into the center chair with a beer. There is an old saying, "Whiskey on beer, never fear, but beer on whiskey, mighty risky." We were drinking beer on whiskey. There is another old saying, "If you drink through the night, don't stop in the morning, you will have less of a hangover."

The center chair is where the wire line, or deep line, is located. Suddenly, Squid had a strike. He said, "Hold my beer!" and gave his reel a couple of turns. He was laboring. "Wait, I have a better idea," he said, "Give me back my beer and you climb in this chair and fight this fish." After 30 minutes I finally landed that big old grouper. Then we landed another and another. When we returned to Pier 5 that evening, we did so with a sailfish, a blue marlin, a hammerhead shark, and plenty of other goodies to boot. We had eventually sobered up, as well. Our sailfish flag was flying as we came back into port, indicating that we had landed one. I called Dad to see if he wanted a mounted sailfish and marlin to hang in the house. Mom said no!

We did absolutely nothing Friday night, except sleep. On Saturday we slept in until noon. Squid and I finally emerged from our rooms in order to eat a nice lunch that Mrs. Brennan had prepared.

"I have hardly had any time to visit with you, Marvin, since you got here," she said, as we gobbled our lunch.

"Sorry Mother, We have just been going, and going."

"You boys were noticeably absent from the house last night. I was worried," she said.

"Oh Mother, you should never worry, we were fine."

"Your mother always worries when you don't come home all night," said Mr. Brennan. "Where were you son?"

"Dean and I went to some club and just lost track of time," said Squid.

"What club?" his mother asked.

"The Vagabonds." He couldn't lie.

"How did you gain entry to the Vagabonds?" she asked, "You are way too young to be going to a club like that."

"Heck Mother, we just walked in."

"Actually, I've been there, the Vagabonds is pretty tame," expressed Squid's father.

"What! We have been married for 22 years, Horace, and you never told me you went to the Vagabonds. When did you do that?"

"Gosh, a long time ago," he said.

"Furthermore, if you think it's tame, what are you comparing it to?"

"Just things I've heard," he said.

"That sounds fishy, Horace, come clean, how many times have you been to strip clubs and
not told me?"

"For heavens sake, Gertie, it's a man's thing. It doesn't have anything to do with me and you."

"It sure as hell does. That's a low down thing to do to me, Horace Brennan."

I could see trouble brewing so I just walked out of the dining room. Squid was right behind me. I certainly was glad that my mom and dad didn't argue, at least Carrie and I never knew it if they did. As the argument in the dining room became more heated, we slipped out and drove to the horse track to watch the races. They wouldn't let us sit where the betting windows were located, but we enjoyed the races anyway. While we were at the track, our conversation once again turned to Miss Mary Ann. "You know Squid. I don't know when I can go to her apartment. I can't check out during the week unless it's an emergency, and I have to spend time with Linda the weekend after we get back. It worries me because I promised to help her."

"Yeah, I know what kind of help she wants," he said.

"Seriously, what should I do?"

"Well, you could call her to see if you can go over there this Monday. We can drive back tomorrow, and you could drop me at Franklin Hall. You could probably get by with staying in our room Sunday night without checking in, and then go over there after mess Monday morning. Whenever you leave her place you could come back and check in."

"Squid, that's a great idea, I'll call Miss Mary Ann."

"Let me know what happens."

"Say, Squid why is the boat we were on called the *Lady Mae*?"

"It's named after movie actress Mae West. I think that my father was infatuated with her. He said that she had beautiful legs, and named the boat after her. Mother got pissed off because we don't have a boat named 'Lady Gertie'."

CHAPTER SIXTEEN

Great Legs

When we arrived back at Squid's house, I reached into that special place in my wallet that had the piece of paper that Miss Mary Ann had given me. I dialed her number. She answered, "Hello!"

"Hi Miss Mary Ann, this is Dean Bass."

"Well hello, Corporal Bass, did you have a nice Thanksgiving?"

"Yes ma'am, how was yours?"

"Oh, it was quite uneventful. Are you still in Miami?"

"Yes ma'am, but I was thinking, if Corporal Brennan and I return to Jacksonville tomorrow then I could come over to your apartment on Monday to help you move furniture."

"Well, that would be wonderful, but I wouldn't want you to alter any prearranged plans that you might have, just for me," she said.

"Actually, we are planning to return tomorrow anyway, so I would be happy to come over Monday, if you still want me to."

"By all means. What time suits you best?"

"How about 10 a.m.?"

"That is fine with me. Do you know how to get here?"

"I can figure it out, I have your address."

"Let me make it simple for you. I live in the apartments located on the side street directly behind Southside High School. Do you think you can find it?"

"Yes ma'am."

"Fine, I'll see you at 10 a.m., Monday morning. Please drive carefully on your return trip."

"I will. Goodbye!"

"Goodbye, Corporal Bass." Miss Mary Ann sounded so sweet on the telephone, I thought.

As Squid and I traveled up U.S. 1 on Sunday, we remembered what the manager at the seafood restaurant told us. We decided to see if he was serious, so when we got to Ormond Beach we stopped in. He was there, and sure enough, he was a man of his word. "Here boys, take this $2.50 and go have yourselves a meal on me, across the street." We thanked him and did exactly that. Once we were stuffed we continued on our way up the highway.

"Which of those two places did you like best, Squid?"

"The first one, because their manager gave us $2.50. How about you?"

"The second one, because it was free."

"It was free because of the first guy."

"Well, we had to pay at the first place."

"Yeah, but that was before we ate so much food."

"Disregarding all that, which was the best?"

"The second, because they had chicken and shrimp. How about you?"

"The first, because they had the best looking waitresses."

An hour and a half later we were at Franklin Hall. I was able to slip in, and up to the room without checking in. I was very careful to cover all possibilities with regard to Miss Mary Ann. I better not call Linda just yet, I thought. If I were to stay at Miss Mary Ann's place for a long time, it might present a problem for me. I wouldn't want Linda to know that I was back in town, because she would wonder why I wasn't anxious to see her. I decided that I should just play it by ear, and see how things went in the morning.

After breakfast, I climbed into Fireball and drove over to Miss Mary Ann's apartment. I was able to wear jeans and a long sleeved shirt because I was still checked out. It was a little chilly outside, but you would never know it by the way Miss Mary Ann was dressed. She opened the door wearing short shorts, I mean short, and a very skimpy halter top. She had bare feet.   I mean those shorts couldn't have been any shorter. "Hello, Corporal Bass, please come in. How are you, and how was your trip back to Jacksonville?"

"Just fine ma'am, on both counts. How are you?"

"I am just fine. I really appreciate your coming over to help me."

"I am very glad to help. You can call on me any time you want to."

"Would you like something to drink?" she asked.

"What do you have?" I inquired.

"I have most any kind of soft drink."

"What about a Grapette?"

"I have NuGrape."

"That's perfect."

She opened two NuGrapes, and we sat down at her chrome, glass top dinette table. As we sat there I could hardly take my eyes off her gorgeous legs. I stared at them through the table's glass top. She sensed that I was staring and said, "Please excuse my attire, Corporal Bass, I have been working around here this morning and wanted to be comfortable."

I got brave. "Miss Mary Ann, if I was staring, I apologize. But you have very beautiful legs."

"Thank you Corporal Bass, I don't mind you complimenting me here at my home, just don't do so in class."

"Yes ma'am."

"Actually, that is one of the reasons that I asked you over. I thought that I might have hurt your feelings when I told you that, after class the other day."

"No ma'am, you didn't hurt my feelings at all. In fact I thought I might have been out of line when I said that if you were my age, or I was your age, I would ask you out."

"Corporal Bass, you were not out of line. I considered it a compliment. If I was your age, or you were my age, and you asked me out, I would definitely accept.

"Really?"

"Really."

"What if you were your age, and I was my age?" I knew that I was pushing it.

"Corporal Bass, if anybody saw us out together, we would both get into trouble. Furthermore, I would probably lose my job."

"Yes ma'am." The thought crossed my mind that she didn't say no.

We sat there for a long time talking about everything imaginable. She laughed a lot, something I had not seen at school. I told her about the seafood restaurants in Ormond Beach, and she seemed very amused. I still couldn't stop staring at her legs, and she realized it. Eventually, she changed the subject back to she and I again, and repeated what she had said before. "Really, if anybody saw us out together it wouldn't be good for either of us." I knew then that the thought of us being together, somewhere, was on her mind.

I pushed a little harder. "Well, we could be friends without going out anywhere."

She took my hand and pulled me up from the table. "Let's move some furniture, okay?"

"Okay," I said, adding, "You said the compliment thing was one of the reasons you invited me over. I assume that moving furniture was another. Is there a third reason?"

"Probably," she said, "I wanted to get to know you a little better, and let's just leave it at that for now. Okay?"

"Okay," I said. Miss Mary Ann either really wanted to change all the living room furniture around, or it was an excuse to invite me over. We moved every piece but one, a Singer floor model sewing machine with a foot pedal. When I saw it, I wondered if she really did raise her hemline with regularity. When we were finished, she gave me a big hug and told me thank you. Maybe I was out of line, but as I was leaving I asked her to please invite me back sometime. She gave me a wink, but didn't say another word. Oh well, I recently got a wink and a hug from Tina before I found out that she wanted my body, so maybe this was an omen.

I had been at Miss Mary Ann's for nearly four hours, and couldn't get our conversation out of my mind. I was in no shape to talk with Linda, so I didn't even call her. When I got back to Franklin Hall, I checked in and went upstairs. Squid was tipped back in my recliner. "Up!" I said.

"Aw, I am so comfortable."

"Well, you are going to want to hear this story, and I tell stories much better when I'm in my recliner."

CHAPTER SEVENTEEN

Love?

The next day, during 4th period English, Miss Mary Ann hardly looked at me. In fact, she hardly looked at me the rest of the week. I wondered if she thought that our conversation had gone a little too far. Well, I told myself, time will tell.

Friday evening, Linda and I went to see *The Blackboard Jungle* with Glenn Ford, Sidney Poitier, and Vic Morrow. After the movie we drove to our favorite "parking" spot in a wooded area on the bank of the Ortega River, to catch up on some overdue love making, which we did.

"I love you!" she said.

"I love you too!"

"I mean, I really love you."

"I mean, I really love you too."

"I mean, I love you so much it hurts."

"I mean, I love you so much it hurts too."

"Why are you repeating everything I say?" she asked.

"Just to emphasize, that I love you as much as you love me."

"That is a very good answer. Sometimes, however, I get the feeling that I am simply a habit with you."

"That's nonsense. I feel sure that I love you as much as you love me."

"Do you really?" she asked. "Feeling sure falls short of being positive."

"Well, I assume so."

"What do you mean, you assume so?"

"Well, I can't tell exactly what you are thinking. I can only assume that you love me as much as I love you based on what you say and what you do."

"You shouldn't assume, you should know. Underline the word know, in your mind," she said.

"You are missing my point a little bit. Okay, I know that you love me as much as I love you."

"More!" she said, "I love you more than you love me."

"That's another assumption."

"If you loved me as much as I love you," she said, "you wouldn't have let out such a big grin at the fair when that girl, Sharon, put her arms around you and kissed you."

"Are you going to keep bringing that up?"

"Well, she is beautiful, and you seemed to enjoy it."

"You're jealousy is showing."

"Furthermore, if you loved me as much as I love you," she said, "you wouldn't have gone to that strip joint in Miami."

"How in the world did you know that we went to a strip joint in Miami?"

"I'll never tell."

"If you really love me, you'll tell me."

"Love has nothing to do with it."

"It has everything to do with it," I said, "people that love each other, confide in each other."

"If that's so, why didn't you confide in me, about going to the strip joint?"

"I don't know. I guess you've got me there."

"I got you there, but that still doesn't answer my question."

"Well, you still haven't answered mine either."

We both laughed, cuddled back up, and dozed off. Three hours later, Linda shook me, "Dean, wake up! Take me home! Hurry! Daddy is going to kill me when I come in this late."

I was sure that I loved Linda. But, that little devil running around in the back of my mind kept me thinking about Tina, Sharon and Miss Mary Ann. I knew I could score with Tina. I was sure I could score with Sharon. And, I hoped I could score with Miss Mary Ann. It had to be some sort of infatuation, I thought. Or, maybe just a need, or desire, to accomplish certain goals. Or, maybe the self-satisfaction that I would get from "conquering" something, or reaching some plateau. That little devil kept egging me on. And, even though she was a little too prissy for me, I was sure that I loved Linda. Although I didn't have anything to compare it with, I was pretty sure that I loved her a lot.

Speaking of love, my buddy Brad caught me in the smoking lounge one day, and said, "Hey Deano, Karen and I are going to get married, and I want you to be my best man."

“Are you shittin' me? When?” I asked.

“January.”

“They won't let you move her into the dorm, you know.”

He laughed, “We are going to get an apartment, and I will change to day status.”

“Are you shittin' me?” I said again. “Karen Marin, Karen Marin,” I repeated. “You know you are going to have to change her first name to Susie, or something else.”

He laughed again, “You will be my best man, won't you?”

“Of course, congratulations, and yes, I would be honored to be your best man.”

CHAPTER EIGHTEEN

The Fire Ax

It really bugged me that Linda knew about the Vagabonds. I could not imagine how she found out. I was certain that she hadn't talked with Squid, and even if she had, he wouldn't have said anything. Nobody else in town knew about it. It really bugged me.

At breakfast Saturday morning, I asked Mom if she could follow me down to the speed shop so I could drop my car off.

"I will," she said, "if you will take Carrie and Sharon horseback riding later."

"What's wrong with Sharon's car?" I asked.

"Nothing is wrong with her car, but her father is holding her keys for two weeks. She was a bad girl. You can take the Caddy, but please be careful with it. No speeding, Dean."

"It's a deal," I said. I took the Plymouth to the speed shop and left it, so they could install all the parts they had ordered for me, and then I drove Mom home in her car. After lunch, Carrie and I picked up Sharon, and then drove out to the Starwood Stables. I parked adjacent to the stable building where our horse stalls were located, unlocked our storage bin, removed the blankets, saddles, and other gear, and the three of us prepared to ride.

The conversation on the trail got a bit personal. "Hey, Sharon, why is your father holding your car keys?" I asked.

"He is punishing me. He didn't ground me. He just took my driving privilege away."

"Why did he do that?"

"I was a bad girl."

"How bad?"

"He caught me fooling around in my date's car, in our driveway."

"Couldn't you have found a better place?" I asked.

"It was just one of those spontaneous things."

"Did he catch you naked, like I did?"

"Just half-naked," she said with a grin, as she spurred her

horse into a gallop.

"Which half?" I asked laughing, but never got an answer.

Carrie was close enough to hear the whole conversation. "You are bad, Dean," she said, and then added, when Sharon was out of hearing distance, "You know, she really, really likes you."

As we eventually rode back in toward the stables, I couldn't believe my eyes. There was Mom's silver Cadillac convertible, up on concrete blocks, with all four of her wire wheels missing. A row of people were sitting on a nearby split-rail fence, laughing and giggling. I knew many of them. I told the girls to be cool, and not say anything. We acted as if nothing was wrong. After we removed the saddles and other gear, we brushed down the horses. A girl that I knew named Sally walked into the building, and as she walked by she said in a very low voice, "Teddy McCormick did it." Carrie and I both knew McCormick. He lived upriver about a mile from us in Ortega. After we had returned the horses to their stalls, I walked over and removed a fire ax from the wall. All stables had axes attached to their walls to assist in getting the horses out in case of fire. I put the ax over my shoulder, and walked straight toward Teddy McCormick, who was one of the giggling people sitting on the split-rail fence.

"McCormick," you have exactly five minutes to get all four of those wheels back on my mother's car, before I start chopping your brand new yellow Chevy convertible to shreds."

"Oh, my God! Don't do that!" he shouted in a panic.

"Time's a wasting!" I emphasized.

"Come on, you guys, help me out." He, and three others, jumped down off the fence and ran into the stable. They had hidden the wheels beneath some hay in a couple of empty stalls. Within seconds they came running out of the building, rolling the wire wheels toward mother's car. They had one jack, so they had to replace one wheel at a time.

"Four minutes, McCormick," I hollered so everyone could hear. Those who were sitting on the fence giggling earlier, were now laughing their butts off.

"Jesus Dean, don't do anything radical!" McCormick yelled.

"Three minutes!" I said. I was not certain that Curtis

Turner's pit crew could have moved any faster, I thought.

"Two minutes before I start chopping, McCormick!" Carrie and Sharon were laughing so hard that tears were running out of their eyes.

"One minute!" I declared.

"Damn Dean, we're almost done, be sensible," McCormick hollered. I had always called him Teddy in the past, but from that day forward I never called him anything but McCormick. As soon as they had finished, he sheepishly walked over to his car, cranked it up and drove off. Nobody ever saw McCormick at the Starwood Stables after that day. I guess his prank had turned into embarrassment. Carrie, Sharon and I sat on the split-rail fence for another 30 minutes talking with everybody before we took off. My thoughts flashed back to that soft little kiss that Sharon had given me at the fair. Maybe it was time to take our friendship another step further.

CHAPTER NINETEEN

The Boathouse

As we drove back into civilization, Carrie spoke, "Sharon, why don't you have dinner with us and spend the night. Neither of us have anything to do."

"I don't have a nightie, my toothbrush, my make up, or hairspray," said Sharon.

I couldn't resist adding my two cents worth. "We have plenty of new toothbrushes, Carrie will give you some make up and hairspray, and the last time I saw you in bed at our house you were naked. So, just sleep naked. Besides, Linda and I aren't going out because I don't have wheels, so I could hang out with y'all if you want me to."

"You are going to run my naked body into the ground, Dean," said Sharon. "Actually, all I really need is a little eye liner, and a toothbrush."

"Does that mean you are going to sleep naked?"

"Hush up, Dean Bass!"

There were three telephone lines coming into the house. Carrie had her own phone, as did Tina, and there was our main line. Dad didn't like it when the main line was tied up very long, so I usually used Carrie's fancy pink phone, with a dial that sparkled, for lengthy conversations. Sharon called her mother to let her know that she was spending the night, and then I talked briefly with Linda. Normally our conversations were lengthy, but this one was very short.

It was customary, in our house, for the employees to eat the evening meal in the breakfast room. Our family and guests dined in the dining room. Whenever we had guests for breakfast or lunch, the same eating arrangements would often prevail. When there were no guests for breakfast or lunch, we all usually ate in the breakfast room, family and employees. Dad was very Bostonian in his ways and everything had to always be very prim and proper. When Dad had business guests, or dignitaries, dinners would be downright formal. So formal, in fact, that on certain occasions, Carrie and I were excluded and would have to dine in the breakfast room. We were usually included, however. During those formal dinners, I was required to wear a tie, and Carrie a fine dress. Blue jeans were strictly prohibited.

It was more impressive, in 1955, to have a white server, rather than a colored one, so Tina would usually serve the more formal meals. She would also serve the drinks and hors d'oeuvres at bridge parties. Sometimes she and Susan would both serve. Even when Squid or Sharon spent the night, things would have to be extremely proper. They both loved it, however, because dinners at the Bass house were always outstanding. Tonight was no exception. We had shrimp cocktails for our appetizers, Greek salads, prime rib garnished with new potatoes, carrots and cooked onions, accompanied by a side of asparagus, soft rolls, and strawberry shortcake for dessert. After dinner we adjourned to the various easy chairs and sofas.

Carrie became engrossed in a horror movie on television, that neither Sharon or I cared for, so I took Sharon by the hand and led her out the back door and down toward the river. Now, when you live on a river, like we did, the front of your house faces the river, or at least it's supposed to. The back of the house therefore faces the street, or at least it's supposed to. Well, Dad always called the street side the front, and the river side the back, so naturally we all had to follow suit. Anyhow, Sharon and I walked out the den door on the river side, and strolled down to the boathouse and dock. Like Carrie, Sharon is a cheerleader at Robert E. Lee High School. She is Lee's reigning homecoming queen, had recently won a teen beauty contest, and is a real looker. Her wavy golden blonde hair is complemented by her stunning light green eyes and a perfect figure. She has an extensive wardrobe, and certainly knows how to dress. What impresses me, also, about Sharon, is that she is very smart, and she loves to have fun.

We talked about her recent beauty pageant, about Lee High, about Kane Military, and several other things.

"That was unbelievable, what you did today with that ax," she said.

"Oh, I really didn't do anything with the ax, it just created an image in McCormick's mind as to what his car might look like if I did start chopping it up."

"That was so neat."

"Thanks," I said. "There is so much bird shit on this dock that it's dangerous to sit down out here, come with me."

I unlocked the boathouse door, flipped on the lights, then took her hand again and helped her aboard our Chris-Craft. I sat down on one of the seats, and patted the one next to me as a gesture for her to sit down. She stepped toward me and turned, then sat in my lap. As she did she draped her arms over my shoulders. It blew my mind. Our eyes were about six inches apart. We just looked at each other without saying a word. God, she is beautiful, I thought. Within moments our lips met. It was the softest kiss that anyone had ever given me. She kept her lips against mine as our tongues darted back and forth. Not only was it the softest kiss, but also probably the longest kiss. My, my, my, I thought, this girl is something else. Sharon's hand went under my shirt, and up my back. My hand went under her blouse, and up her back. "Unhook my bra," she said, and I did. She rotated my hand around to the front. Lord, her breasts felt good. "Make love to me, Dean." Those words brought me back to earth.

"Sharon, I would love to, but not here. Somebody is liable to miss us and come looking for us."

"I want you."

"I want you too."

"Can you sneak into my room tonight, after everybody is asleep?"

"Baby, it's too risky," I said.

"I'll be naked and waiting, if you'll come."

"Look, I can tell, making love to you would be phenomenal, but this isn't a good place to do it. Somebody could catch us here in the boathouse, and somebody is liable to hear us in your guest room."

"I want you so much," she said

"We'll do it soon."

"Promise?"

"I promise." Here I was, making promises again.

I locked the boathouse back up, and then put my arm around Sharon, and we strolled back up the lawn to the house.

When we entered the den, Carrie started laughing.

"You had better wipe off that lipstick, big brother, before the folks see it," she said.

CHAPTER TWENTY

The Dunes

Somehow I was able to avoid a discussion with Tina during the weekend. My car wasn't ready, so I got Dad to take me back to school Sunday afternoon. I ascended the tower stairs and found Squid sitting in my recliner with another comic book. I flopped down on my bottom bunk, and told him about Sharon and the boathouse.

"You're a lucky shit, but you had a chance to poke her and you didn't," he said.

"It's just a matter of time," I said.

"Say, what's the latest on Wanda?"

"I talked to Linda about that, and it is a go for Friday night."

"Fantastic!"

"Speaking of Linda, how in hell did she find out that we went to the Vagabonds."

"I can answer that question," said Squid.

"Well, spill."

"Remember, we left Miami a day early. Well, Linda called my house to talk to you. Mother answered the telephone and told Linda that we had left. Then somehow during their conversation she let it slip that she was upset because we had gone to a strip club."

"I couldn't imagine how Linda found out. But that explains it."

"I apologize for my mother."

"Hell, it's one of those things."

"That's great about Friday."

"Yeah, it looks like you're finally going to get laid."

"Yep, I get to break in the back seat of your new car."

"Nope!"

"Why nope?"

"My car is in the shop, so we have to take yours."

"Why is your brand new car back in the shop?"

"I already told you, I am having some speed equipment installed."

"Oh yeah, I forgot," said Squid. "Well, the condoms are in my glove box, so they are ready, when I am ready."

"Great," I said. "Plan to stay at my place next weekend."

"Thanks!"

"We still have a couple of hours of daylight left, so let's go throw the football around."

"Okay!" he said. I reached into my footlocker, removed my football, and we headed to the field.

As we skipped down the stairs, and passed the second floor, I noticed something that I had not seen before. Howard Hill's door was open and I couldn't believe my eyes. Hanging on one of his walls was a large Nazi flag. We stopped, and I pointed it out to Squid. I stepped to Hill's door. He was sitting at his desk.

"Hey, you guys got me in trouble with that beer the other night," I said.

"We didn't do anything to get you in trouble," Hill said.

"Absalom saw one of you walk out with a bottle."

"Sorry man, we didn't mean any harm,"

"What's the deal with the Nazi flag?" I said. "The war was over ten years ago. Are you a Nazi sympathizer?"

"No, it's just a World War II memento. A reminder of the tragedy that our soldiers went through," Hill said.

"But, a Nazi flag? It just doesn't make sense to display a Nazi flag. Furthermore, you aren't supposed to put something that large on the wall," I said.

"I got permission," said Hill. Squid and I just shook our heads and continued down the stairs.

"That guy is definitely weird," I said.

"I agree, he's very strange," said Squid.

Squid and I saw a couple of new boys outside the main lounge, and a neat idea popped into my head. "Brooks," I said. "You live on my side of town. I want you to do me a favor next weekend when you check out."

"Yes sir!"

"Do you know Teddy McCormick?"

"I know of him, and where he lives, but I really don't know him," said Brooks.

"Here is a five dollar bill. Use it to buy as many rolls of toilet tissue as you can. I would prefer pink rolls if you can find them. But white will do if you can't find pink. I want you to "tree" McCormick's front yard. There are four or five large trees in his yard, and I want you to do a good job of draping them all with tissue. Do it late at night after their house lights are off.   Do you think you can handle that?"

"Yes sir!" responded Brooks.

"If for any reason you get caught, don't mention my name. Do you understand?"

"Yes sir! Consider it done."

Maybe it was my imagination that Miss Mary Ann was ignoring me in class, because during 4th period on Monday she seemed to look at me a lot. Actually, that trend continued Tuesday and Wednesday, as well. When the bell sounded to end our class on Wednesday, she motioned to me with a nod of her head. I knew she wanted to talk to me, so I lingered behind the others.

"Corporal Bass, I have several of William Shakespeare's plays on records from the Shakespeare Recording Society," she said. "Being that we are studying Shakespeare, I thought you might like to come over to my place and listen to one with me."

"Yes ma'am, I would love to." Actually, I wasn't crazy about Shakespeare, but it was an invitation I couldn't refuse.

"How about this Friday night?" she asked.

"Ma'am, I have plans, could we do it Sunday night?" It crossed my mind that I had said, do it.

"Sunday night would be just fine, Corporal Bass, how about 7 p.m.?"

"Yes ma'am, 7 it is."

Squid flipped out when I told him about my conversation with Miss Mary Ann. "We need to check you back in Sunday afternoon," I declared. "I'll check out until Monday morning, and that way I can come back in anytime Sunday night."

"Or, Monday morning, if you get lucky," said Squid. He was pumped up about his date with Wanda. Squid was finally going to have sex. "Where are we going Friday? Should we rent a room somewhere? Or, two rooms."

"Let's play it by ear," I said. "If it's not too cold, we'll take a couple of blankets and go to the dunes. If it's too chilly, we can go to plan B."

"What is plan B?"

"I don't know, but we'll think of something."

I called Mom to let her know that Squid would be spending the weekend. She indicated that Sharon would be there also. "Carrie would like to speak to you," she added, and handed the phone to Carrie.

"Dean, I need a huge, huge favor," Carrie said. "Sharon, still doesn't have her car back, and all the cheerleaders need to be at the big Lee High pep rally Saturday night. We're in the championships you know. There is going to be a huge bonfire. We will be doing cheers and the band will be playing, and it will be fun. Will you please take us?"

"I don't know Carrie, let me think about it," I said.

"Dean, you know most of the cheerleaders because you drove us in two parades last year, we need a ride, and besides you have never seen us doing our routines, except in the back yard. I really want you to go, and so does Sharon. Pleeeeeease!"

"All right!" I gave in. "Squid and I will take you."

"We need to be there by 6:30 p.m., okay?

"Okay, I'll enjoy watching you cheer."

"Thanks a bunch, Dean. You are sooooo sweet."

"Okay, okay, I don't need any molasses."

Friday arrived quickly. Squid and I checked out, and then went to my house to change and have dinner. After dinner we drove over to Linda's house. Wanda lived in Tampa so she was spending the night with Linda. It was a little windy but not very chilly, so we agreed to give the beach a try. Linda gathered up some blankets and a cooler with a few soft drinks and a little beer. Then, we drove to my favorite isolated spot south of Jacksonville Beach.

The public parking lot was completely empty. We pulled in and cut off our lights. Linda and Wanda got the blankets and cooler from the trunk and we crossed the dunes to the flat sand by the ocean. I told Squid to give us two beers and take the cooler. They walked north and we headed south. After laying the blanket on the beach, we came to the conclusion that the wind was blowing too much sand, so we decided to climb toward the top of the dunes. We could look down toward the parking lot from our vantage point, and with the light from the half-moon we could see Squid's car. Evidently, they had come to the same conclusion regarding the wind, and headed to the car. They climbed into the back seat.

"Eureka," I told Linda, "Squid is fixing to lose his virginity."

"I know that's been a priority of yours," she said as she laughed.

Here I was with Linda, but for some reason I wasn't interested in making love. As we gazed toward the parking lot, we noticed a car pulling in slowly with its lights off. "I wonder why that car has its lights off," I uttered.

"That seems so strange, and scary." responded Linda. "Is that the police?"

"I can't tell. It's too dark."

All of a sudden two extremely bright flashlights shined into Squid's car, one from each side. We could hear Wanda's scream from the top of our dune. Once the lights went on we could see that it was the police. After a few minutes, the cops turned their flashlights off and returned to their car. They put their headlights on and drove out of the parking lot. Meanwhile, Squid had cranked his Ford up, turned on his headlights, and was leaning on his horn. We gathered up our stuff and walked down to the parking lot.

Wanda was freaking out. Not knowing that we had seen what happened, she said, "Two cops sneaked up and scared the piss out of us. I was nearly naked, and Squid was putting a condom on, when they shined their lights through the windows. I guess they got an eyeful." We could see that Wanda was still trembling. Squid didn't say a word. He got out of the car and unlocked the trunk so we could put up our things. Wanda climbed up front, and Linda and I got into the back seat.

"Well, we can go find another spot," I suggested.

"Not on your life!" Wanda proclaimed. "I am a nervous wreck. Let's go back to town."

We did just that. After stopping at the Polar Bear Drive-In for a bite, we took the girls to Linda's house.

"Tomorrow is Saturday. Are we going to do anything tomorrow night?" Linda asked.

"I guess not. I promised Carrie that I would take her to the Lee High pep rally."

"So, I guess that means we're not going to make love this weekend at all. Right?"

"Linda, we make love all the time. It isn't going to hurt to miss one week."

"Dean, we definitely do not make love all the time. I went to Ocala one weekend, you had Bull Ring another, and then you went to Miami for the Thanksgiving holiday. Lately, we have only gone out one evening on those weekends when we are both in town. And, this was a very short date tonight."

Linda was not very happy. When she gets into moods like this, it is always better to just walk away. I didn't want to get into a "discussion" with her, so I didn't say another word. I leaned over and gave her a little goodnight kiss, without an embrace. Wanda and Squid said their adieus, and we took off.

"You two don't seem as happy as you did a year ago," said Squid.

"You are probably right," I added. "She is a great girl, and I love to be with her, but evidently some of the magic is gone from our relationship."

CHAPTER TWENTY-ONE

The Pep Rally

As Tina passed me in the hall on Saturday morning, she grabbed my butt. "When?" she asked.

"Soon," I said, not having any idea when that would be.

After breakfast, Squid took me to the speed shop so I could pick up my car. As I left one stop light on Hershel Street, with Squid following me, I couldn't resist. I stomped on the gas and Fireball leaped into action. I ripped the Hurst shift into second in a swift speed shift, and then let off the gas. Wow, that is exactly what I wanted, I thought. I now have a very quick machine. I drove by Joe's Standard Service on Ortega Boulevard. An acquaintance, named Junior, had been building a hot rod in Joe's garage. Squid and I parked, and walked inside to talk with him.

"Junior, I've got something for you to test that rod against when you get the finishing touches put on it," I said.

"Yeah, I heard you got a hot runner. Is that it out there?"

"That's it."

"Let me go see it." We walked outside. He raised my hood, and said, "Yeah, it looks like it might run. When I get through with mine, let's take them out to Thunderbolt." Thunderbolt was brand new, Jacksonville's first drag strip, and anybody could go out there and practice.

"Hell, we'll just get it on right here on Ortega Blvd," I said.

"Anywhere you say."

"It's a challenge!"

When we arrived back at the house, Carrie asked if we could go get Sharon, so we did. We ate a late lunch, or maybe it was an early dinner because it was the only meal we consumed before the pep rally. Squid sure got googly-eyed when he saw Carrie in her cheerleading outfit. It's possible that my reaction was similar when I saw Sharon in hers. We left the house at about 6 p.m. so we would get to Lee High in plenty of time. Maybe I was prejudiced, but the girls at Lee seemed much better looking than the ones at Southside High, or at Hobart. With the exception of the times when the girls had to do their cheers, Sharon was all over me the whole evening long. She introduced me to zillions of people, none of whom I will remember. The rally was nice, and fun. Somebody had gone to a lot of trouble to stack a great deal of wood for the bonfire. The Lee majorettes twirled their batons, and the band played on. As the night wore on, it became much colder. Sharon snuggled up to me as close as she could get. Gosh, it was fun being with her. We had all four of our arms wrapped around each other, when suddenly somebody tapped me on the shoulder. I turned my head, and my heart sank.

"Hi Peachy, how are you?"

"Fine! I can see that you are fine too," she said sarcastically.

"This is Carrie's best friend, Sharon, and Sharon is cold, so I was trying to keep her warm. Sharon, this is Linda's friend, Peachy. Peachy-Sharon. Sharon-Peachy."

There was even more sarcasm in her voice when she said, "Dean, it looks like you are doing a good job of keeping Sharon warm. Nice meeting you Sharon." With that she turned and walked away. I still held onto Sharon tightly.

My eyes followed Peachy as she walked clockwise part of the way around the bonfire. She stood by some guy I had never seen, but her eyes kept looking over at us. Sharon watched her also, and when she saw Peachy looking our way she turned and kissed me. Oh, that was clever, I thought. This girl can definitely be devilish. I put my forefinger on the bridge of her nose, and then slid it down across her cheek and back to her chin. "You are so beautiful," I said.

"I love it when you touch me like that," she said, as our lips met again.

Well, I was sure that Linda would hear all about it, later tonight or first thing in the morning. Sharon had my undivided attention, however, and my heart was fluttering like a butterfly.

"How can your lips be so soft," I asked Sharon.

"Dean, I want you to make love to me tonight."

I saw Carrie and Squid sitting on a wall nearby, so I steered Sharon over that way. "Hey y'all, Sharon and I are going to the car. Just hang out here for at least 30 minutes, before you head to the car, okay?"

"Okay," they both said.

The car was parked in the middle of the parking lot. We opened the right side door and climbed into the back seat. We were both naked from the waist down in about five seconds. She made love to me with vigor, with intensity, with emotion. And, those soft lips just put me on cloud nine. Lord, she was exceptional. We fogged the windows up so fast that nobody could have ever looked inside.

"Damn, that was fantastic!" I said, as I noticed her putting bikini panties back on.

"That was incredible!" she declared. "We should do it every chance we get."

"I agree completely." After we got dressed we cracked the windows in order to unfog the inside, and then walked back across the parking lot. As we did so, we passed a Studebaker that was swaying back and forth. Its windows were also all fogged up. We found Carrie and Squid sitting in the same place we had left them. They both had big grins on their faces.

We went to the Tepee Drive-In to eat a little something on our way back to the house. The building is round, and the roof looks like a real tepee. The waitresses deliver the orders on roller skates, so it is a fun place to eat.

Sunday morning, I tried to call Linda. Her father indicated that she and her mother had gone to St. Theresa's. I left a message for her to call me. When I didn't hear from her, I called back a little later.

"Dean," her mother said, "Linda has informed me that she doesn't want to talk to you."

"I can understand that. Please tell her that I called." Hell, I thought, I wonder how bad Peachy made things sound. Linda knew I was going to the Lee High pep rally. Maybe she thought there was a reason that I didn't ask her to go with me. She was jealous because of the kiss that Sharon gave me at the fair, and she knew that Sharon would be at the pep rally. Was it just a coincidence that Peachy was there? Well, maybe Linda will come around, I told myself. After that call, however, the thought also ran through my mind that maybe I should move on, and forget about Linda. Well, hell, I might not have any choice in the matter anyway.

Linda is definitely pissed off. So far, she hasn't confronted me for an explanation of my actions. If she does, I don't believe I could even give her a logical excuse.

I couldn't get my mind off of the great love making session in the Lee High parking lot. It is said that first time sex with anyone usually leaves room for improvement. Well, if that's the case I can't wait for the second time because Sharon was unbelievably good.

Squid and I took a spin up the road to check out Teddy McCormick's yard. Brooks had done an awesome job. All of the trees were heavily draped with pink, blue, and white toilet tissue. With no rain in the immediate weather forecast, I imagined that the tissue paper would last for many days. We got a great laugh out of that, as others probably did also.

Late Sunday afternoon, Squid headed back to school and I left a couple of hours later to go see Miss Mary Ann.

CHAPTER TWENTY-TWO

Shakespeare

English is one of my favorite courses. It isn't because we are studying Shakespeare. It is because of the incredibly gorgeous teacher that I was on my way to see. I arrived at Miss Mary Ann's at precisely 7 p.m.

The door opened, "Hello, Corporal Bass. How are you this evening?"

Once again, she was dressed to blow my mind. "I am fine, Miss Mary Ann. How are you?" She was wearing short shorts again, but these were sexier. There was a large brass ring on each side that exposed a lot of skin. The top she was wearing was nothing more than a silk scarf wrapped around her boobs and tied in the back. It was thin and her nipples projected slightly through the fabric, like a magnet for my eyes. As before, she was barefoot. She sensed that I was staring and she just kept smiling.

"I hope you don't mind my attire, Corporal Bass, I like to be comfortable around my apartment."

"Not at all Miss Mary Ann, you can be just as comfortable as you want around me." I can't believe I said that. Was that corny, I thought? "I have told you before that I think you are very beautiful. Actually, I think you are very sexy also." Golly, I thought, I can't believe I said that either.

"Do you really?" she said, "Do you really think I'm sexy?"

"Absolutely!" By now I was certain that she liked to flaunt it a little, so I thought I would try to take it to another level. "Miss Mary Ann, with all due respect, and I hope you don't take this wrong, but I love to look at you, and if you find me staring, it's because I think you have an incredible body."

"Thank you Corporal Bass, you have my permission to look at me as much as you wish, and I hope you don't mind if I look at you in return. Would you like a NuGrape?"

"Yes ma'am. Thank you ma'am."

"Shall we listen to some Shakespeare?"

"Absolutely, I love Shakespeare." I lied.

"What is your favorite Shakespearian play, Corporal

Bass?"

"*King Lear* ma'am, but if I am going to sit here with you for a couple of hours I would prefer a love story like *Romeo and Juliet*, because you definitely intrigue me."   Damn, she's an English teacher, I thought, intrigue isn't the best word to use.

"But, *Romeo and Juliet* is a tragedy," she said, "and please tell me Corporal Bass, how do I intrigue you?"

"Miss Mary Ann, again with all due respect, you arouse my desire, you - you, well to be very frank, you turn me on."   Lord, I thought, I can't believe I said that either.

"Corporal Bass it pleases me that I turn you on, and being that this is confession hour, I must confess that you appeal to me, as well."

"Thank you ma'am, that's nice to hear."

"Now let's listen to Will."

"Yes ma'am." She put on *Romeo and Juliet*.

After one side had played, she asked, "Corporal Bass, if I lie on my tummy here on the sofa would you rub my back."

"Yes ma'am, I would be glad to."   Without switching the record to its flip side, she lay down on her stomach, then reached behind her and untied her top, or scarf, or whatever it is. She folded her arms under her head exposing the sides of those awesome boobs.   She was definitely blowing my mind.   I started high, rubbing her neck, then her shoulders, and then I massaged her back slowly up and down and slightly around her sides, but as much as I wanted to feel the sides of those boobs I was afraid to do so. Then I got brave. I slid my hands over her shorts to the tops of her legs. When I did so she moaned.   It was a moan of approval. I massaged her legs all the way to her ankles. Then I lightly rubbed her butt again, and got another moan.   This time as my hands worked their way back up her back they drifted down to the sides of her huge jugs.   She let out another moan.   "That was wonderful, Corporal Bass, thank you very much."

"Would you like a front rub?" I bravely asked.

"That might turn me on too much, and I get very weak when I get turned on excessively. But thank you for offering. Possibly another time."

"I would do anything to please you, Miss Mary Ann."

"Anything?"

"Yes ma'am, anything."

"I'll definitely remember that. Will you tie my top?"

"Yes ma'am." Well that was as far as we went, but I felt very confident that I would be invited back again soon.

As I was leaving, she leaned forward and gave me a little kiss, then said, "Corporal Bass if we were to have a relationship and anyone ever found out, it would ruin me. Do you understand?"

"Yes ma'am, I understand. I would love to have a relationship with you, and nobody would ever know. Nobody! I think we would both enjoy each others company."

I left her apartment and drove back home. I decided that I should honor her wishes and not say a word about anything, not even to Squid.

From that day on, I made a habit of lingering behind as 4th period let out, just so I could say a few words in private to Miss Mary Ann. That seemed to please her.

I took Sharon out the following Friday and Saturday. She was so much fun to be with. I still hadn't heard from Linda, and was beginning to care less whether she called or not. Tina still wanted me, and I convinced myself that I should find time for her. It complicated matters because Sharon spent so much time at the house.

Miss Mary Ann met me at the door that Sunday night clad in almost nothing. I knew immediately that I was going to score. She opened the door wearing only a short shear black nightie, and no panties. When I saw that see-through nightie, I knew she was ready. I took her hand and led her straight to her bedroom. There was very little foreplay. We wasted no time getting right to it, and then talked later.

CHAPTER TWENTY-THREE

Southside High

Crawfish brought back several thousand feet of green and yellow streamers from New Orleans, so I put my re-curve bow and two dozen old arrows in my trunk. I told Miss Mary Ann what I was going to do, and she decided to give me a little limited help. From her patio, the following Sunday night, I shot 24 arrows, with either green or gold streamers attached, over the roof of Southside High School, completely draping their school with our school colors. She thought it was, as she described it, a "cute" prank. Brad's sister attended Southside High. She later advised us that most of their students got a big laugh when they arrived at school Monday morning. Oh well, it was a tame prank, but we had to retaliate in some manner for some of their past "deeds."

There is a concrete sign where the driveway turns in from the highway to Franklin Hall. On its face, are mounted three rows of black iron letters reading Kane Military Academy. Two days after I shot the streamers, the letters on the sign had been painted pink. I thought, those guys are all day students. They can go do damage anytime they want to. It is much more difficult for us to retaliate. Miss Mary Ann was probably right, I thought, the streamers were "cute." I also thought, however, that we needed to do something more substantial. It was time to come up with a solid foolproof plan. The night after the entrance sign turned pink, several of us met in Fulton Dames' old quarters after study period. Crawfish had a key.

We agreed upon one plan and put it into effect the following Saturday. Zebra and Brad and a few others went out to a salvage yard on Tallyrand Avenue. They bought an old wreck of a station wagon for 50 dollars, and then painted it green and gold. Then they hired the salvage yard to tow it, on Sunday, to South-side High and deposit it across the sidewalk in front of the main entrance. We thought it was a funny idea, but we heard through the grapevine that the school administration simply called another salvage yard to pick it up. The salvage yard paid the school $25 for the wreck, which was put into the school bank account. So, that prank wasn't too effective. Two or three days later the cannon and bottom of the flagpole in Hard-ass Circle were painted in a rainbow of colors.

Well, we met again to come up with new ideas. Zebra called a gravel company, told them he was so-and-so with Southside High School, gave them a purchase order number and requested delivery of a truck load of gravel to be delivered on Sunday and dumped right in front of the main entrance to the school. Evidently, the gravel company didn't question the order one bit, because a truck load of gravel blocked the main entrance steps on Monday morning.

"I should have ordered five truck loads," Zebra said. "That was too easy."

Brad's sister was able to do a little "spying" for us at Southside. Their band was scheduled to march in the Christmas parade in downtown Jacksonville. The band always rode in two buses to their destination. Their tubas, drums, and other instruments were always transported by a third bus. Brad typed up elaborate instructions on an SHS letterhead that his sister was able to obtain. The instructions gave specific directions on what route to take to get to the City Hall parking lot in Jacksonville Beach, 15 miles to the east. Brad and Zebra mixed in with students outside the band room the morning of the parade.

After the bus carrying the instruments was loaded, Brad approached the bus driver, and said, "The band director asked me to advise you that the other buses would be slightly delayed, and for you to go ahead. He said to give you these directions and that you would know what to do." The whole thing was very iffy, and any number of things could have gone wrong, but the driver cranked up the bus and departed.

The Southside High School band marched in the parade as planned, but did so without their instruments. Furthermore, their majorettes were lost without the beat of the band to do their strutting and baton twirling. I can attest first hand, because I drove Mom's silver Cadillac in the parade, with the top down, and the Robert E. Lee cheerleaders sitting all over it. Sharon stood on the hump right next to me, holding on to the windshield and waving to the crowd. Carrie was sitting on top of the back seat with several

other cheerleaders. For a couple of hours, I felt like a big cheese.
As we rounded one corner on Forsyth Street, I spotted Linda in the
crowd. I waved to her, but she just looked at me and didn't wave
back. Anyhow, the prank worked, and was probably the best that
we had done so far.

After our last two escapades, there wasn't any immediate
retaliation by Southside High. Maybe that meant that we had won,
at least for the time being.

CHAPTER TWENTY-FOUR

Thunderbolt

Well, needless to say, I liked fast cars and fast women. It seemed as though I was having much more fun with Sharon than I ever had with Linda. Sharon was just great to be around, and she always gave me her undivided attention. She was more of a free spirit, and fun loving, but I would still think of Linda once in a while. I had dated her for many months and it was hard to get her out of my mind. She was sweet and usually understanding. I guess she had labeled me a cad. Sharon had a more bubbly personality, knew more people, and was more outgoing. We definitely enjoyed each others company, and the sex was amazing. She was Carrie's best friend, and I sometimes wondered if my sister was driven by sex as much as her best friend was. Carrie was more verbal about this guy or that guy being "so good looking." Sharon never said anything like that around me.

Miss Mary Ann is another story. She and I would usually get together once a week, for sex, and talk. It had become a routine. We couldn't be seen together out anywhere, so the sex was always at her apartment. I was still interested in getting together with Tina, because I knew that it would be for sex only. Also, I was sure it would be quite good.

Junior finally finished working on his hot rod. It was sleek and loud. Basically, it looked like an engine with four wheels and a seat. He was all smiles one Saturday when Sharon and I pulled into Joe's Standard Service. "Are you ready to go?" he asked.

"Absolutely," I said.

"What about tomorrow morning, at Thunderbolt? The gate will be unlocked," he said.

"Name the time."

"11 a.m."

"It's a go, I'll see you there."

"Deal!"

I was able to get word to Squid, and Rooney, and my friend Ray who had a Pontiac powered Corvette, because I knew they would want to be there. Squid showed up with Crawfish,

Zebra, and Brad. Carrie rode to Thunderbolt with Sharon and me. Junior had just as many friends present, including Joe from the station. Joe and Zebra walked down to the finish line to authenticate the winner.

Sharon stood between the cars at the starting line in order to give the go signal. Junior and I revved our engines. I could see Carrie standing to one side clapping. I got the level of rpm's that I wanted. Sharon lifted her hand in the air, and then thrust it down. Fireball leaped forward, and I speed shifted into second, and then third, as I ran away from Junior.

"Dean, I didn't get good traction. My wheels did too much spinning," said Junior. His rod was light and developed too much torque too quickly, causing his lack of traction.

"Okay let's do it again," I said. We lined up on the starting line again. Sharon gave the signal again, and I beat him badly once more. Junior was so disappointed. He had worked on that hot rod for months, and my Plymouth ate him up. He wanted to go a third time, so we did, with the same results. Junior was embarrassed.

"Hey Dean, let's try it one time in reverse," he said.

Reverse is geared even lower than first gear, so you can not go fast very far. Also, your steering is controlling the following wheels, not the leading wheels, which makes it much harder to direct your car. "I'll go you once in reverse," I said. Junior seemed to have better traction in reverse, but I beat him again.

"Shit, this just isn't my day," he said.

"Next you'll be wanting to play chicken," I said.

"No way, your machine would crush this light rod."

"Your right, no way, only idiots play chicken. Besides I wouldn't want to put a scratch on this paint job."

Sharon had a big grin on her face. "I love fast cars," she said.

"What about the driver of a fast car? Do you love him too?" I asked.

"You know I do," she said.

"I don't know that. You have never told me."

"Well, Dean Bass look me straight in the eye. I love you," she emphasized.

"Awesome," I said.

"What do you mean awesome? That's not what you are supposed to say when I say, I love you."

"What am I supposed to say," I said with a grin.

"Well, if you don't know, I'm disappointed," she said.

"Sharon, look me straight in the eye. I love you very much."

"That's better!" she indicated, as she put her arms around me and gave me one of those super soft kisses.

Ray walked up to me, and said, "That was very impressive. But are you ready to taste defeat?"

"The main reason I bought this car, was so I could whip your Vette." I still don't know how Ray put that Pontiac engine between the fender wells of his Corvette, but he did. The carburetor stuck up in the air so high that it blocked a lot of his vision when he drove. I had been in that car with him many times and I knew that it was fast.

"Should we make a wager on the outcome, and then run 'em out?" he said.

"How much would you like to bet?"

"Ten bucks!" he indicated.

"You're on!" I said. We lined up side by side, with Sharon between our front bumpers. This time Carrie and Rooney were at the finish line. I watched the rpm's on my tachometer as I got my revolutions up. When Sharon's hand came down, Ray and I charged off the line neck and neck. When I did my speed shift to second gear, I moved slightly ahead. Another speed shift and I was comfortably on my way to victory.

Back at the starting line we both exited our cars. "Very impressive, very impressive," Ray reiterated, as he reached in his wallet and pulled out a ten dollar bill. With Sharon standing beside me, Ray said, "By the way, I like your new girlfriend a lot better than your old one."

"Thanks, I do too."

Sharon threw her arms around me and gave me another kiss.

CHAPTER TWENTY-FIVE

Panty Raid

Sharon asked me to the Christmas dance at Lee High. I bought her a pretty orchid corsage for the occasion. She was absolutely the most attractive girl at the dance. It was great that we had our Christmas vacation coming up, because it would allow us to spend much more time together.

Kane Military had to be back in school for class on January 10th, but Hobart resumed classes on January 3rd, one week earlier. When Linda and I had been dating, we thought that the 8th or 9th would be the best days for Kane to stage a panty raid on Hobart. She was going to open the second floor dormitory door to the fire escape, and the boys would all dash through the dorm collecting panties. Well, Linda isn't speaking to me now, so another plan needs to be devised. I discussed the matter with Sharon. She said, "That's not a problem. I know several Hobart girls who will open that door for you. You tell me exactly when you want the door opened, and I am sure I can get one of my friends to oblige."

Lord, that was simple, I thought. After talking with Zebra and Brad, and some of the other guys that lived in town, we agreed that 8 p.m. on January 8th would be the time to have the door opened. Squid indicated that he did not want to miss the action, and that he would return early from Miami. Some of the others stated that they would be back early also. We estimated that we might have between twenty and thirty guys. Sharon expressed a desire to go, but to wait in the car while it was going down. The plan was firmed up. All those going on the raid would wear jeans and black sweat shirts, and meet at Handy Amby's Drive-In at 7 p.m. on the 8th. Sharon later advised that she had two friends, Babs and Brenda, who were going to man the door at 8 p.m. Everything was set.

Sharon and I exchanged presents early. She bought me a suede jacket, and I got her a cashmere sweater and skirt to match. I bought Miss Mary Ann six pair of bikini panties from Frederick's of Hollywood, and had them shipped directly to her. I didn't want to have to explain to Mom or Carrie what I had ordered from Frederick's, so I didn't have them sent to the house. Miss Mary Ann had a very nice knit sweater waiting for me on one of my visits. From that night when she opened the door dressed only in her short shear nightie, she never came to the door again dressed in anything more. It was all about sex and we had good sex.

The Christmas holiday came and went too quickly. Sharon and I spent a great deal of time together. One day, we went to St. Augustine, the nation's oldest city, which is just south of Jacksonville. We spent hours just walking around, arm in arm, in the historic district. I was amused when we passed a gift shop called the Vagabonds. We had both been to St. Augustine many times before, but never together, so it was special. While we were there we crossed the river to Anastasia Island and the St. Augustine lighthouse. We climbed the 219 steps to the observation deck, and then sat up there for a while looking at the sights.

One night Sharon and I were on Ortega Blvd., possibly moving along a little too fast, when I saw a patrol car's red light some distance behind me. "Shit!" I said, "He can't catch me."

Ortega Blvd. was straight as an arrow until it curved left as it went out toward Ortega point. I flattened the accelerator to the floor, and put more distance between him and us. Once I rounded the curve and couldn't see the patrol car, I told Sharon to hang on. I cut the headlights, yanked the emergency brake up, spun my doggie knob to the left, released the emergency brake, and popped the lights back on, all in the same motion. I spun the car around 180 degrees, and then drove slowly past the cop in the opposite direction. He glanced at me as he went flying on around Ortega point, and we never saw him again.   "That was amazing!" declared Sharon.

"Are you all right?" I asked.

"Sure," she said. "How did you do that?"

"Well, I'll explain the maneuver. The emergency brake locks the brakes quickly, and it doesn't activate the brake lights, so the patrolman was not able to see any brake lights. The headlights and taillights have to be off or they will reflect off of the trees and houses while the car is spinning."

"Interesting! Let's go get a beer!"

"Okay!"

Sharon and I went to three Christmas parties prior to Christmas day. Two were mild, and one was wild. It was really wild. Several people started removing their clothing about midnight, so we eased out the front door and headed elsewhere.

The two of us attended mass on Christmas morning, and then we went to my house for a lavish dinner. Mom, Carrie, and Tina all helped Susan make the necessary preparations. It was a meal that would make any chef jealous. On the following day, I cranked up the Chris-Craft and took Sharon south on the St. John's River. We found a quiet little cove, dropped anchor and made fantastic love.

By a strange coincidence, Sharon received an invitation to a New Year's Eve party at Linda's house. Somebody obviously didn't make a connection. We assumed that some of Linda's friends at Hobart helped her put the invitation list together. Sharon had several friends at Hobart. We got a good laugh out of that. So, did Carrie and the folks. While Linda was having her party, Sharon and I were quietly curled up on a sofa at my house watching the ball drop at Times Square on the new color television that Dad had bought for Christmas. The old black and white console that was in the living room was moved to the den and the den black and white went to Dad's bedroom. There was a new 30 foot antenna in the yard. Only a few shows were in color, but how great, I thought. Dad was always one of the first to have anything new. We were very fortunate.

Sharon started back to school at Lee on the 3rd of January, so I didn't see much of her that week. Suddenly, it was upon us. It was time for the panty raid.

The dormitory at Hobart is a long narrow two-story building. There is an exterior fire escape at each end, and an interior stairwell about 40 feet from each of the ends. The entire second floor consists of dorm rooms, as does about 3/4 of the lower level from the west end. There is a dining room and kitchen at the east end of the first floor. Our plan is to climb the fire escape at the east end. Babs and Brenda will see that the second level door is open. We will all run down the hall collecting as many panties as possible, take the west interior stairs to the first floor, run past the other dorm rooms, eventually exiting through the dining room door at the front of the building, near the east end. When we met at Handy Amby's we took a head count. There were 31 of us, plus one woman, Sharon. Squid didn't make it back from Miami in time.

At precisely 8 p.m. on January 8th we rolled into Hobart. There were five guys in each of six cars. Sharon and I took Fireball, so we could do something after the raid. Well, everything went as planned. The guys climbed the fire escape. I kissed Sharon and then brought up the rear. Two girls were at the second floor door to greet us. I assumed it was Babs and Brenda. The girls were all standing by the doors to their rooms, waving panties in the air. I guess we hadn't done a very good job of keeping the raid a secret. Each of us grabbed the panties as we ran down the hall.   Then it was down the stairs to the first floor, and more girls, and more panties. The guys ran down the hall, then made a right turn into the dining room, where we were supposed to exit from the building. As I ran down the first floor hallway, Wanda grabbed me and pulled me into her room.

"Dean, the police are corralling everybody in the dining room. Climb out my window and run. You should be safe," she said.

"Thanks Wanda!" I said as I exited through her window. I dashed to the car and jumped in, then drove to the other side of the parking lot to sit and watch. None of our guys were leaving the building.

"What happened? asked Sharon.

"I don't know. The police are in there."

"I don't see any police cars," she said.

"They must have hidden them." I drove around the classroom building and sure enough there were two patrol cars sitting there. I stopped about fifty feet away, got out and ran over to the cars. They were both empty. I opened a front car door of one. The keys were in the ignition. I quickly removed them. Then I removed the keys from the ignition of the other car. I noticed a canister of tear gas clamped to the dashboard, undid the clamp, grabbed the tear gas and dashed back to my car. I drove around to the back side of the dining room near the kitchen entrance, got out and tried the door. It was unlocked. I snuck in through the kitchen, activated the tear gas and hurled the canister into the dining room. As I did so, I yelled, "Tear gas! Run!"

With four patrolmen right behind, the guys all bolted out the front door. They leaped into their cars and laid a lot of rubber as they squealed away from Hobart. Two of the cops ran to get the police cars while the other two stood out front. I jumped back into my car, but couldn't leave the premises without driving right past those two policemen. Sharon was a lifesaver. As we drove slowly around the east end of the building, one of the cops flagged us down.

"Hello," I said, "is there a problem?"

"What are you doing here," he asked.

"Oh, my girlfriend here is a Hobart student. She and I are going to the movies."

The cop shined his flashlight into the car and saw Sharon clearly. "Sorry," he said, "You may proceed."

"Thank you, sir!" I said, and we drove away slowly. I was sure everybody would be able to get away, because I had thrown the keys to both police cars into a thicket of shrubbery.

"Did you see Linda in there?" Sharon asked.

"No, she was noticeably absent," I said. Then I told her about Wanda and what she had done. We headed back to Handy Amby's Drive-In, but none of our guys were there. We decided to do what we had told the cop we were going to do. We went to the late feature of *Love is a Many-Splendored Thing*, starring William Holden.

I checked in at Franklin Hall nearly two hours prior to classes on the 10th, changed into my uniform and then walked down to the smoking lounge. I was bombarded by questions from some of the fellows that had participated in the panty raid.

"Where did you get that tear gas? How did you get into the kitchen? Why didn't you get caught? Why didn't we see any police cars? Where was your car when we left? Who do you think set us up?"

I just smiled and said, "Guys, I have no idea what you're talking about." I put out my Chesterfield and walked out of the lounge.

I didn't see Squid until 4th period English. "I'm glad I didn't get back to Jacksonville in time for the panty raid," he said. "But, I have heard all about it."

After class, I lingered behind to talk to Miss Mary Ann. "Are we on for Sunday evening?" she asked.

"Absolutely," I indicated.

"7 p.m.?" she inquired.

"I'll be there!" Actually, for the first time, I was beginning to feel a little guilty about our relationship. Then I would remind myself that it was just sex, and the guilt would disappear.

That evening during study period, Squid asked, "How did Wanda look?"

"How did you know that I saw Wanda?" I was surprised, because Sharon was the only person who knew that Wanda had helped me during the raid.

"She told me."

"When did you talk to Wanda?"

"Last night, when I got back," said Squid. "The night that we went out, she had given me four phone numbers to the pay phones in her dorm. I have been thinking. My best opportunity to get laid is probably with a girl who has already agreed to screw me. So, I was able to reach her, and we talked for a while."

"Next time you talk to her please tell her that I said thanks for helping me."

"Okay. Guess what else I found out?"

"What?"

"She said that she was pissed off at Linda, or she wouldn't be telling me this, but Linda had told the matron at their dorm about the panty raid and the matron called the police. Together they decided to set a trap."

"Thanks for filling me in," I said. I was really disappointed in Linda. I couldn't believe she ratted on us. She sure could get pissy about things. It was just as well that our relationship was over, I thought. "Are you going to take Wanda out again?"

"We agreed to go out, but we haven't set a date yet. Say, I hear you are a real hero around here."

"What are you talking about?"

"You know, the tear gas."

"I don't have a clue what you're talking about."
Squid just grinned.

CHAPTER TWENTY-SIX

Bachelor Party

I still thought about Linda occasionally, but in a negative way. It bothered me that she had blown the whistle on us prior to the Hobart panty raid. That panty raid didn't happen at all like I thought it would. When we charged into their dorm, it was supposed to be a surprise. Those girls were just waiting on us with panties in hand. The element of shock wasn't there. They were supposed to be astonished by the bravado of the raid, and I had imagined all those horny girls lifting up their skirts and removing their panties as we ran through their dorm. It sure didn't happen that way. I guess we didn't plan it very well.

Wanda sure saved the day over at Hobart, I thought. If she hadn't pulled me into her room, and let me out her window, we might all have wound up at the police station. I was glad that she was talking with Squid. She might be the best option to get him laid. If that didn't happen fairly soon, I had another option. There was a new whore house that I had heard about called the Green Beacon. It was located on the northwest fringe of town. When the beacon was green, the coast was clear. When it was red, there was no entry.

I was a little surprised that the police never came by Kane Military after the panty raid. At least they didn't to my knowledge. They obviously knew that it was Kane students that made the raid. Maybe they were embarrassed that we all escaped, that they didn't have keys to start their patrol cars, and lost a canister of tear gas in the process.

Brad's wedding was approaching. Saturday night, the weekend before, was the only time we could schedule a bachelor party for Brad. As best man, it was my responsibility to do the planning. Bachelor parties sometimes have a tendency to be a little rowdy, so I rented a hospitality suite at the Sandpiper Inn, a motel just outside of town on U.S. Highway 1. The suite had a large living room, a bedroom, kitchen and bath. It was perfect for a group of about thirty, which is about how many we had attending. Most of the guys were KMA students, but there were a few others that were some of Brad's closer friends. The owners of the Sandpiper Inn knew that we were going to have a party, so they charged me an extra five dollars cleanup fee.

Zebra, Crawfish, Squid and a couple of others, each chipped in a few bucks on the beer kegs and the hors d'oeuvres. I kept the stripper a secret, except from Squid, and sprang for the expense myself. Well, every bachelor party should have a stripper, and most do, but I didn't want anybody to necessarily know about her, even if they asked.

I know a fellow named Leonardo that owns a topless bar in downtown Jacksonville. The law allows topless dancing, but not totally nude dancing. Leonardo would often have one of his girls dance completely in the buff. Naturally, she would be arrested. He would immediately bail her out of jail. The newspaper would have a story the following day, and people would flock to Leonardo's bar. It was his way of keeping his establishment packed with patrons. It was a successful routine that he did over and over.

Leonardo was a classy bar owner. He lived on our side of town, in a very nice mansion on the St. Johns River, and attended our church on a regular basis. At least he always seemed to be there when I attended, which was only periodically.

I had a dentist appointment one afternoon, and was excused from school. After Dr. Baker finished filling a cavity, I headed to Leonardo's bar. He was in his office and I was invited in.

"Leonardo, I need one of your best looking girls to strip at a bachelor's party. I need a honey that will take it all off. Can you help me out?"

"Certainly Dean, how is your family?"

"Just fine, sir." Although he seemed to be a good Roman Catholic, Dad and Mom didn't especially like Leonardo. They were always very cordial to him, but didn't respect him because of his business and the way he conducted it.

"That's good. Do you want a girl that will also turn a trick for a price?"

"Sure, but I wouldn't want her screwing anyone at the party except for the groom. It would be his decision whether he wanted to or not. Is that okay?"

"Anything you want. I will send a girl named Sugar. You pay me. I will pay her. If she and the groom partake of any other deed, pay Sugar. Please see that she also gets a healthy tip from the fellows at the party."

"I will, and thanks. If there is any extra-curricular activity, please tell Sugar that I will pay her for it, not to charge the groom." I reached into my wallet and gave Leonardo some cash. He wrote down the date, place, suite number and time, 10:30 p.m. Everything was set.

I knew the party would probably last into the wee hours, so I scheduled it to start at 9 o'clock. That way we could get in a little poker and some serious beer drinking before Sugar arrived. Most of the guys were very prompt and showed up on time. Squid picked up Brad to assure that he would be there. The party went according to plan, until there was a knock on the door at about 10:00 p.m. I opened the door. There stood a plump, squatty little old lady, probably in her fifties. She was cockeyed. When one eye looked at you, the other seemed to derail. Her hair was pitiful. It was brown with reddish-orange stripes running through it. It was definitely worse than Zebra's. She had a huge nose and two big warts on her left cheek, with hair growing out of both. I hate to judge people, but she had to be one of the ugliest women that I had ever seen.

"I am supposed to ask for Dean," she said. My eyes drifted to the several holes in her stockings.

"I'm Dean."

"Well good, I am ready to go to work. Sorry I'm early. I'm Sugar."

I couldn't help but smile. Somebody was playing a trick on me, and it had to be one of two people, either Leonardo or Squid. They were the only ones that knew that I had hired a stripper. Squid rarely ever took the initiative to do anything on his own, so I was fairly sure that Leonardo was putting me on. I decided to go along with the jest. "Please come in Sugar," I requested. "Boys, this is Sugar. She is a stripper and she is going to dance for you." Squid looked shocked. I found out later that he thought I was pulling another of my pranks. But bless his soul, he went right along with it and started clapping. The other guys, including Brad, seemed amused and also began clapping. There was a stack of records on the phonograph that I had borrowed from Carrie. I turned up the volume. *Hey, Bo Diddley!* by Bo Diddley was playing. Sugar, or whoever she was, commenced dancing. The old broad had some pretty good moves, and the guys were all egging her on. "Take it off!" was the cry. She began to strip. She removed her blouse and skirt as she danced. Beneath them she was wearing a thirties style, one-piece bathing suit. It looked hideous with those dreadful stockings and her pudgy rolls of blubber. "Sorry boys, that's as far as I go," she exclaimed. She put her blouse and skirt back on. The guys were all good sports and tipped her a few dollars. She thanked them and departed.

Less than five minutes later there was another knock on the door. Once again, I answered. This time there was a tall, well built, sexy looking lady standing there with a grin on her face. "Are you Dean?" she asked.

"I am."

"I'm the real Sugar. How did you enjoy Leonardo's humor?"

"Oh, I think we got a kick out of it. Where did he find that woman?"

"Isn't she pathetic? She is a homeless beggar named Bertha. Leonardo feels sorry for her, so he hires her as a joke to do just what she did for you. I drove her over here and waited in the car. Now she will wait while I do my thing, but she won't mind. She's a little richer."

I invited Sugar in. "Hey guys, say hello to the real Sugar. Sugar, this is the groom, Brad. The rest of these drunks, that I don't claim, are his friends." She had to repeat for the others what she had just told me about Bertha being homeless, and her boss trying to help the poor gal out. Actually, Leonardo's stock in my book just went up. It's a nice gesture to help her, and a funny gag.

Sugar is a real professional. She certainly knows how to tease while she dances. The motion of her body was captivating. As soon as she was topless, and had stripped down to just her G-string, she climbed into Brad's lap. Sugar buried Brad's head between her tits as she wiggled and waggled, and he squirmed. Yes, he definitely squirmed, but his ear-to-ear smile indicated that he was enjoying it. Eventually, she pulled off her G-string, and was as naked as a new born baby. Seeing that I was holding some cash, she approached me next. I gave her a tip with my left hand as my right hand gave her left boob a little squeeze. The other guys took note, and immediately reached for their wallets. Sugar got plenty of tips, and her tits got plenty of squeezes.

"Say Brad," I said, "there is a king-sized bed in the next room if you and Sugar want to continue the fun."

"Karen would kill me if she ever found out. I'll pass."

The group hollered, almost in unison, "Henpecked!"

Well, Sugar was only there for a little over an hour, but she was definitely a hit. The last keg ran dry about 3 a.m., so all of the inebriated party goers headed home.

CHAPTER TWENTY-SEVEN

Brad's Wedding

Bones Gifford was in the infirmary, so Brad took command of our platoon for drill the following week. As usual, when he assumed the position of platoon leader, he marched us to the woods for a lengthy cigarette break. It was Wednesday.

"Hey Brad, when you get hitched and switch to a day student, are you still going to be second in command of our platoon?" I asked.

"Yeah, except one of you squad leaders will substitute for me during formations when I am absent."

"Are you getting cold feet? Are you going to back out?"

"I can't back out. You have committed to being my best man, and it wouldn't be fair to you, for me to back out," he said.

I laughed, and then added, "Just four days and you will join the ranks of the unavailable. Where is your new apartment?"

"It's in the complex directly behind Southside High School," he said.

Oh shit, I thought, that's where Miss Mary Ann lives. That could present problems. "Have you furnished it yet?"

"It's half furnished, both my folks and her folks are helping out. We'll have it looking pretty good in a couple of weeks, I hope."

"Karen Marin," I said. "That cracks me up."

"I told her what you said about changing her name to Susie, or something else, and she thought that was funny. Say, my sister will have my car, can you be at my mother's house by 3:45 p.m. Sunday, and take me to the church?"

"Sure, no problem."

Well, Sunday was upon us. Sharon and I went to Brad's mother's house at 3:45 p.m. as he had instructed, to pick him up. We couldn't believe our eyes. Brad was walking around the side of the house carrying two garbage cans to the street. He was dressed in jeans and a sweat shirt.

"Are you still getting married in 15 minutes, or did you cancel it?" I asked.

"I'm getting married in 15 minutes. Come in and help me

with my studs and cuff links."

We arrived at the church five minutes late. Karen's mother and Brad's mother were both in a panic because we were late. Karen's brother, Tank, who had a long red beard and many tattoos, was the leader of a motorcycle gang. He was also an usher in the wedding. In his life, he had never worn a tuxedo. And, his gang had never seen him "dressed up," so they all rode their choppers to the wedding to view the spectacle.

There was a weird combination of people in the church. On the groom's side were the mayor, city councilmen, Major and Mrs. Harden, businessmen, and all those who didn't want to sit with the motorcycle gang. On the bride's side was the motorcycle gang all wearing their black leather, rivets, and chains. One of the mommas was wearing a black vest with its two sides held together by a little brass chain. There was nothing under it. The biker sitting next to her had his arm around her, with his hand neatly tucked inside one flap of the vest.

Well, needless to say, everything went just fine. They both said, "I do." The wedding reception was at a nearby garden club. Karen and Brad had known beforehand who was coming to the wedding so they were prepared. At one end of the room was a champagne fountain. At the other end were two large tubs, filled to the brim with cans of cold beer. Brad and Karen had prepared well, and everybody was happy.

While the happy bride and groom were standing next to each other in the reception line, I snuck behind them and clamped a set of police handcuffs on Brad's right wrist and Karen's left. They were locked together. As the reception wore on, and they begged to be unlocked, I assured them that I had no key, and that they were locked together forever. The wedding photographer snapped some great pictures of Karen and Brad feeding wedding cake to each other with the shiny silver police handcuffs dangling between them. It was hilarious when they attempted to hoist two champagne stemware glasses to each others lips. It was a very sloppy maneuver. Most of the champagne wound up on the floor. Naturally, Karen was still in her wedding gown, and Brad in his tux. Finally, when it came time for them to change clothes and hit the road, Karen was beginning to get distressed. Certain that I had carried my little prank as far as I could, I gave in and unlocked the cuffs.

During the reception, I had a chance to speak to Major Harden.

"Sir, have you had any news regarding the whereabouts of Wilhelm von Kreisler?"

"I have not! Nor has his father. I speak with him often and he has not heard a peep from his son since he left school. We fear that the worst might have happened," said the major.

"I hope not!"

"I appreciate your concern, Corporal Bass. I will let you know if I hear anything."

"Thank you, sir."

I had gotten a tip that Brad and Karen were going to the Ponce de Leon Motel in St. Augustine for their honeymoon, so four car loads of us made a beeline to St. Augustine and arrived there ahead of the newlyweds. I had to hide my car because it stood out anywhere. We waited, and waited, and finally they arrived. Brad went into the office and checked in, and then they drove to their room, removed two suitcases from the trunk, unlocked the door and disappeared. Within about ten minutes their light went out. We waited another five minutes before I knocked on the door. "Room service!" I said, trying to disguise my voice.

I could hear Brad's voice through the door, "Damn, it's Deano!" After a few minutes they opened the door. We were all standing there with three bottles of champagne. For the next half hour we partied with them, before we eventually realized that we really were intruding, so we departed. By the time I got Sharon back to Jacksonville it was getting late, so I drove her to her house.

CHAPTER TWENTY-EIGHT

Trouble for Miss Boobs

Squid and I were sitting at our desk during study period one evening the following week. As usual, he was reading another *Dick Tracy* comic book. I was reading *The Album of Gunfighters*. I looked up from my book.

"Don't you ever get tired of Dick Tracy?" I asked.

"Nope!"

"Who is Tracy chasing this time?"

"He is in hot pursuit of Pruneface," said Squid. "Say, who is your father supporting for President?"

"Eisenhower," I said. "How about your dad?"

"He would like to see Senator Estes Kefauver win the democratic nomination."

"Why Kefauver?" I asked.

"I think it's because he headed up the Kefauver Committee investigating organized crime, and Miami is a mafia hot bed," said Squid. "I rather imagine that Adlai Stevenson will win the nomination again, and then get trounced by Ike like he was during the last election."

"I agree. It's too bad we can't vote yet," I added.

Suddenly Joseph Absalom walked in. "Corporal Bass, Major Harden wants to see you in his office, immediately."

I knew something must be terribly wrong because Hard-ass never stayed in his office after 5 p.m., and here it was, past 7 o'clock. I made a beeline for his office, walked in, and snapped to attention with a salute. He returned my salute, saying, "At ease Corporal Bass. Close the door, and have a seat here beside my desk, I want to talk with you."

"Yes sir!"

"It has been brought to my attention, that several cadets have been spending time at the residence of Miss Mary Ann Tolliver. In fact, I have a list of five names, and yours is one of those on the list, Corporal Bass. I have interviewed three of the others, all day students. I would like to know what you and she do when you are at her residence for several hours. Please keep in mind that I am not accusing either you or her of doing anything underhanded, I am just trying to protect the image of Kane Military Academy. Do you understand?"

"Yes sir, absolutely."

"Furthermore," Major Harden added, "The information that I have comes to me from very reliable sources, so it is in your best interest to level with me, shoot straight, and tell me the truth. Do you understand that, as well?"

"Yes sir, absolutely."

"Kane Military Academy was founded in 1948. Our school is an honor military institution, with an impeccable reputation. That reputation is important to the future success of this institution. Do you understand?" Major Harden was raising his voice more and more as he continued to talk.

"Yes sir, absolutely."

"We work very hard to make Kane Military Academy the wonderful school that it is. It makes my blood boil when I hear something that I think might tarnish the fine reputation of this institution. Do you also understand that?" His face was turning red, and his voice was at a high pitch.

"Yes sir absolutely. May I speak, sir?"

"Speak, Corporal Bass, speak, but tell me the truth. I know you are making A's so don't tell me that you are over at her residence being tutored. And, I don't want to hear one of your manure stories again. Go ahead and speak!"

"Sir, Miss Tolliver is a very fine English teacher. She is so wrapped up in her work here at Kane Military, that she takes it home with her. It is important to Miss Tolliver that we, as students, learn as much English literature as possible. She has a fine collection of long playing records from the Shakespeare Recording Society, that have a great many of William Shakespeare's tragedies, comedies, and histories. Miss Tolliver has taught us to appreciate and love the works of the greatest playwright the world has ever known. When I am at Miss Tolliver's residence, we listen to Shakespeare and drink NuGrape. Miss Tolliver is a very fine English teacher, sir."

"Corporal Bass, believe it or not, I once went to high school. When I was in high school, everybody hated Shakespeare. Now, you boys all come in here and tell me how much you love Shakespeare. Should I really believe that?"

"Yes sir, absolutely. It's an indication of how good our teacher is, sir."

"You may return to study period, you are dismissed, Corporal Bass."

I walked out of Major Harden's office thinking, five names huh, Miss Boobs must be a sex maniac.

Miss Mary Ann was in class the following day, as usual. After class, I told her exactly what happened. She indicated that she had already heard. She also indicated that Major Harden had instructed her to meet with him after classes. Miss Mary Ann thanked me for saying what I said to Major Harden.

I had to know the outcome of their meeting, so I called Miss Mary Ann early that evening. As always, there was a crowd around the pay phones. I told Miss Mary Ann that I couldn't talk, but I could listen. She told me that the major was very cordial during their meeting. However, she said, he emphasized several times that he thought it was inappropriate for a female member of the faculty to invite students of the opposite sex to her residence, and suggested that she terminate the practice immediately. She told him she would. But, the last thing she said to me was, "You mean a lot to me Corporal Bass, we'll think of a way around this." I hung up the telephone wondering if she told the other four guys on the list the same thing.

CHAPTER TWENTY-NINE

Nude in the Cookery

Sharon and I went to see a Little Richard concert on Friday evening, then spent two hours at my favorite parking place, in the woods, above the bank of the Ortega River. It was always soft lips, naked bodies and extraordinary love making.

Saturday morning Dad drove me to the Jacksonville Police Pistol Club on the north side of town. We were both members, and had signed up to participate in the best pistol match of the year. Both of us won medals, Dad in Expert Class, and me in Sharpshooter Class. There was a lot of competition so we were both very pleased.

Mom convinced Dad and Carrie to accompany her to early mass Sunday morning. Susan wasn't due to arrive until 10 a.m., so when I awoke, I went down to the kitchen to grab a little breakfast. Tina was standing by the stove fixing herself a cup of coffee. She was wearing the same robe that she dropped in order to show me the first bikini panty that I had ever seen.

"Good morning, Tina!"

"Good morning, Dean!"

"Are you wearing a bikini under your robe?" I couldn't resist.

"Would you like to see?" she asked.

"Sure." I said.

She untied her belt slowly, as if to tease me, and then let her robe drop to the kitchen floor. There was no bikini. Tina was naked as a jaybird. She took my hands in hers, and then wrapped my arms about her placing my hands on the cheeks of her butt. Her lips met mine as we pressed our bodies against each other. She sure knew how to give a wet, sloppy kiss. My hands raced all over her body. Tina reached over, picked up her robe, and cut off the burner on the stove. She guided me into her quarters, locked the door behind us, and then quickly peeled my robe and pajamas off. I had never experienced so much foreplay. Not even with Miss Mary Ann. Tina certainly knew how to please.

"That was excellent!" I said, after we had finished making

love.

"Damn it Dean, we could have been doing this for months. Look at what we have missed out on," she said.

"I know, I know, but it's been difficult to find time, especially since I have been dating Sharon." The thought of Sharon caused me to sit up, and put my pajamas and robe back on. Other thoughts ran through my mind like, I guess I am a real cad, and, maybe I should substitute Tina for Miss Mary Ann, after all they are about the same age.

I went back upstairs and jumped in the shower. Shortly thereafter, Carrie and the folks came home from mass. "I assume that you went to St. Theresa's, right?" I asked Carrie.

"We did!"

"Did you see Linda there?" I couldn't believe that I even asked that question.

"We did!"

Tina was a cool girl. She and I got it on a couple of more times over the next few weeks, and she never seemed a bit jealous when Sharon was at the house, which was often. It was just a sex thing with her, like it was with Miss Mary Ann. She would cut up and have fun with Sharon and Carrie, just like one of the girls, which of course she was.

Speaking of Miss Mary Ann, she and I had not gotten together since right after the Christmas holidays. I sort of missed all the rendezvous. One day after 4th period, I suggested that we might meet at a motel sometime, and she seemed very amenable to the idea. I tucked the thought away with every intention of bringing it to fruition.

It had been a while since I'd been to Thunderbolt, but that didn't hinder my love for drag racing. There was always the street. It was indeed exciting when two fast cars stopped at an intersection together, revved their engines and popped their clutches as the light turned green. I had the fastest car in town and everybody knew it, so I got plenty of challenges. Sharon loved speed, and seemed to get a thrill every time we squared off against another fast car. Junior did some rebuilding on his hot rod, but when we cranked it up on Ortega Blvd., the result was the same. I never raced against Ray again. Eventually, he got tired of his Vette, sold it, and bought a Nash Rambler that was extremely slow.

I gave Sharon a dozen red roses and a box of chocolates, with a large bow on top, for Valentine's Day. We attended the annual dance at Robert E. Lee High. The gymnasium was nicely decorated with huge red hearts, and red and white balloons and streamers. I never realized just how popular Sharon was until that night. It seems as though everybody in the gym talked with her at one time or another during the evening. I knew the cheerleaders and a few other people that were there. She introduced me to the rest. Sharon sure knew how to make a guy feel good. Whether she was or not, she seemed very proud to be with me. She stuck to me like glue all evening and wouldn't even dance with anyone else. What a super female! Why, I wondered, was I messing around with any other girl.

CHAPTER THIRTY

Elvis and NASCAR

Elvis Presley was going to be in town for concerts on February 23rd and 24th, a Thursday and Friday. Squid and I knew that we would have difficulty checking out from school on Thursday, so we purchased four tickets for the 24th. The Grand National Stock Car race on the beach in Daytona was two days later, Sunday the 26th. So, we bought four tickets to the race also. It was going to be a very busy weekend. Squid and I knew that we couldn't get into trouble, especially after making plans and buying tickets. It would be terrible to have Bull Ring that weekend and be confined to KMA. We knew that it would really disappoint the girls also.

Presley had a huge new hit on RCA Records, *Heartbreak Hotel.* The song was written by Mae Axton, a resident of Jacksonville. Her son attended Robert E. Lee High School with Sharon and Carrie. Sharon and Squid both spent the weekend at our house. Squid and I took Sharon and Carrie to the concert. Elvis performed at the new stadium, downtown. There had been a riot at Elvis' Jacksonville concert just seven months earlier, so the place was packed with policemen. He had been told to restrain from suggestive gyrating on stage, but he didn't know any other way to perform. Girls shrieked, shouted, and cried, and when the concert was over there was almost another riot. It was an amazing concert. In just a matter of months Elvis Presley had gone from an unknown to the most popular entertainer in the country.

Squid was crazy about Carrie, and loved to be with her. Carrie, on the other hand, liked Squid as a friend, but seemed romantically cool toward him. And, Squid was not one to make advances toward any girl, especially his roommate's sister, so they never even held hands. Not at an Elvis Presley concert, or anywhere else.

Saturday, we took my .30-06 out to the rifle range. Squid wanted to learn how to shoot, so I taught him. He learned fast. Within a couple of hours, he was peppering the targets with a fairly tight group. The girls went along to watch. In fact, they were so patient, that we decided to do something for them, so we took them out to the Starwood Stables to go horseback riding. We rode for about two hours, put the horses up, and pointed Fireball toward the house. On the way back home we stopped for strawberry sodas, and to let Squid pick up a new supply of *Dick Tracy* comic books.

With both Sharon and Squid at the house, dinner Saturday evening was again very exceptional. We had an appetizer of cold vichyssoise, followed by a ginger salad, then porterhouse steak, scalloped potatoes, carrots, asparagus casserole, biscuits, and an apricot compote for dessert. I had two huge helpings. Carrie, Sharon, Squid and I hit the hay early because we needed to get an early start the next morning for Daytona.

As we drove south on Sunday morning, I gave the girls a little preview of what we were going to witness at Daytona Beach. Squid had already heard most of what I said.

"We are going to Daytona Beach to see the Grand National Stock Car Race. The track is half on the beach and half on Atlantic Avenue at Ponce Inlet, which is as far south as you can go without driving into the Halifax River. It is a 4.1 mile oval track. The start-finish line is on Atlantic Avenue. The race is 160 miles, or 39 laps long. Some of the best drivers anywhere compete in this race. Drivers like Curtis Turner, Lee Petty, Tim Flock, "Banjo" Matthews, Marvin Panch, Cotton Owens, and Joe Weatherly."

"I've heard of Curtis Turner." declared Sharon.

"When we get there, we want to get a good vantage point near turn 3, because the best action is there. The cars will approach us, heading from south to north along the two mile beach stretch. As they approach turn 3, they will be gearing down, and sliding sideways, before taking the ramp to Atlantic Avenue. During the progression of the race, the cars will actually dig a large hole as they spew the sand at that turn."

"Will we get covered with sand?" asked Carrie.

"No, we won't be that close to the action," I said.

As we headed down U.S. Highway 1, we passed the two seafood restaurants in Ormond Beach where Squid and I had dined to and from Miami three months earlier. The restaurants reminded me of that trip.

"Hey Squid, did your mother ever get over us going to the Vagabonds?"

"Hell Deano, I don't know. She and my father argue all the time. It wouldn't surprise me if they got a divorce."

"Sorry Squid, I shouldn't have brought it up."

"No sweat man," Squid said.

"It's too bad that they argue," chimed in Sharon. "I'm glad that Dean and I have never had an argument. I bet we never argue when we get married someday."

Wow, I thought, that is the first time either of us has mentioned that possibility. She must really love me. That's nice!

We had left Jacksonville very early to assure that we would get to Daytona in plenty of time. In fact, we were quite early, so the four of us walked on the beach north of the track for about an hour and a half before we settled in to watch the race.

There were 76 cars competing in the NASCAR event, with a lot of fender bending that made the race very exciting. Tim Flock took the checkered flag, in his 1956 Chrysler. His winnings totaled $4,025.00.

On our way through Ormond Beach we stopped at the seafood restaurant where the benevolent manager worked. The meal was good. I asked for the manager just to let him know that we were bringing him a little business. I was informed that he had gone to the stock car race, and was not there. It was just as well. He might have wanted us to dine across the street again.

I had Brad and Karen's address in my wallet and was anxious to see which apartment they had rented, so upon our return to Jacksonville we turned in to the complex behind South-side High. They lived in an upstairs unit in the building next to Miss Mary Ann's apartment. Lordy, Lordy, I thought. If I were to visit Brad, somebody might see my car and think I'm at Miss Mary Ann's. If I were to visit Miss Mary Ann, then Karen and Brad might see my car and ask questions. My initial reaction was that I should stay away from there, at least for a while.

CHAPTER THIRTY-ONE

Tribulations

Squid finally arranged a date with Wanda. It was a strange date. She didn't want him to pick her up at Hobart. And, she told him that she was meeting him for sex. He was to go to Cherry's Deluxe Cottages, and rent one of their cabins, and then park his car directly in front of his cabin. She would be along shortly, spot his Ford, and knock on the door. Well, as he conveyed the story to me, everything went just fine with the check-in process. He got his cottage, parked his Ford in front, twenty minutes later Wanda knocked on the door and he let her in. She gave him a peck on the cheek and started to undress. He also started to undress. Wanda was down to her bra and panties, and he to his under drawers when somebody started pounding on the door.

Wanda ran to the window, peeked through the curtain and the jalousies, and then turned around in horror. "My God, it's my boyfriend Jake. He must have followed me over here. He's a bad one. You don't want to mess with him." According to Squid they were dressed in a flash and he was sitting in a chair when Wanda opened the door. When her boyfriend stormed in and wanted to know what the hell was going on, Wanda saved the day again. "Hi Jake!" she said. "I want you to meet my cousin, Squid. He called Hobart to let me know he was in town, and wondered if I could come over here to see him. I told him yes, that I would be right over." Not trusting Wanda, Jake asked Squid why he was driving a car with a local tag. Squid replied that it was a rental. He went on to tell me that he thought Jake had his doubts about the whole thing, and that he grabbed Wanda by the arm and escorted her out the door. As they left, Jake told Wanda to tell her cousin goodbye.

As we sat at our desk in Franklin Hall, Squid's sad story gave me an idea. I scanned the newspaper until I came to the personal ads, which I read slowly.

"Squid, listen to this personal," I said. "It reads, 'Lonely, attractive redhead seeks relationship with a gentle, considerate guy in his twenties. Must have car. Please call me at 555-7493. I am waiting.' Shit, it sounds like she is primed and ready to jump in the sack, right now. Go downstairs and call her. Set something up."

"Damn Deano, I'm not in my twenties," said Squid.

"She is not going to know that when you call. If she's horny, like the ad indicates, she probably won't care how old, or young, you really are when she sees you. Call her!"

Squid went down to the phones, and returned thirty minutes later. "Deano, she didn't even ask me my age. We plan to meet at MacDonald's on Phillips Highway, Friday evening. You know, the place that has the two yellow neon arches, and the sign that says, 'Over a million hamburgers sold.' I'll need to use your address, to check out."

"See how easy that was," I said.

"Now I'm nervous about it. I get apprehensive when I have a blind date. What if she's ugly?"

"You can't go wrong meeting at MacDonald's. If you don't like her looks, you can call it off, and vice-versa."

"You're right! It can't hurt to meet her. Her name is Pat. She said she would be wearing a hot pink blouse so I would recognize her."

I was anxious to see Sharon, so I checked out at school and headed home for the weekend as usual. I told Sharon about the ad in the personals, and that Squid had called and arranged a date with a girl named Pat, in hopes of getting laid. Sharon and I spent Friday evening at my house. It was a treat to watch a television show in living color. With Dad's thirty foot antenna we were able to pick up a show from Atlanta, with pitiful reception, but in color. Saturday, she, Carrie, and I went horseback riding during the afternoon. Carrie had a date that evening with some guy from Lee High. Sharon and I went to a party at Rooney's house. I picked up two six-packs and put them in his refrigerator. Naturally, I washed Fireball before going to Rooney's place because I knew he would want to show everyone there the marvelous custom job that he had done on my car. I was right, he showed everybody his handiwork. Of course, that made me proud as well. There were a lot of people there, mostly liquor drinkers, but our beer disap- peared after we only had two each. So, we didn't stay very long. We were anxious to go make love, so we headed to the Ortega

River overlook.

I drove back to Franklin Hall late Sunday. Squid was sitting in my recliner reading a *Terry and the Pirates* comic book.

"What is this?" I asked. You are always reading *Dick Tracy*. I have never seen you reading a *Terry and the Pirates* comic."

"I have to broaden my horizons," said Squid.

"How did your date with Pat go?" I asked.

"Shit, you would not believe it."

"I would, tell me."

"Well, I walked into MacDonald's and there she sat in her hot pink blouse, so I sat down beside her on the bench seat. She was tall but not ugly. She leaned over and kissed me on the cheek, then took my hand and placed it right between her legs. I yanked my hand back immediately, and stood up. Would you believe, she was a he. A shit-eating female impersonator. A guy, with a high pitched voice, dressed up like a girl with make-up, hair spray, and all. I declared to her, or him, that I was not interested, period, and then went straight to the men's room to scrub the lipstick off my cheek. When I came out, that impersonating faggot was gone, thank goodness. Damn, I felt sorry for Squid. How many times was this, I wondered, that we attempted to get him laid, but didn't? Poor Squid. I realized that the time had come for us to take him to the Green Beacon.

CHAPTER THIRTY-TWO

Green Beacon

We didn't even plan it. The first opportunity we had, Zebra, Crawfish, Squid and I took off for the northwest side of town. It was a Friday evening. I called Sharon to tell her what we were doing. She laughed and said almost the same thing Linda had once said, "You are going to wait out front, right?" One of the guys in the smoking lounge had drawn us a very detailed map. We were determined to get Squid laid. He had been a virgin long enough. On the way we stopped at a Gulf station to get him a new condom, just in case he needed it, and then continued on our way.

As we drove along, it occurred to me that I, a Bass, was riding in the same car with two other underwater creatures, Squid and Crawfish, and a mammal, Zebra. They had quite strange nicknames, for certain.

The Green Beacon was nothing more than two old white frame houses sitting side-by-side, in a wooded area just beyond a subdivision. There was a green light in the window of the one on the left. We could barely see a couple of cars out back, but there were none in front. We parked out front, but not too close.

"Okay Squid, can you do this by yourself, or do you need moral support?" I asked.

Squid had gotten much braver since our trip to the County Line. He probably thought nothing could be as bad as that guy Jake, or the impersonator, ruining his week. "Hell, I'll go in there by myself if I have to. You don't think they have any Doberman pinschers in there do you?"

"Naw!" we all echoed.

Squid got out of the car and walked to the door of the house on the left. They invited him inside. About ten minutes later he walked out the door with a girl. It was too dark to tell what she looked like. They walked over to the house on the right and entered.

"Well guys, it looks like Squid is finally going to get laid," I said.

"Amen!" they concurred.

Within minutes, three vehicles came creeping toward the houses with their lights off. It was dark, but it looked like two police cars and a paddy wagon. We slid down in our seats, as they crept past us.

"Oh, shit! They are going to take Squid to jail," said Zebra.

"Shit, shit, shit!" said Crawfish.

"I don't believe this. Stay down, so they don't see us," I said.

Several cops got out, and headed toward the left house. When they were all on the porch together they burst into the house in unison. We found out later that by a bell signal of three quick rings the left house notified the right house of a raid.

Squid came running out of the house on the right, butt naked and holding his pants. I had never seen him move so fast. As Squid neared the car, I cranked up Fireball while Zebra rolled down the front right window. Squid threw his pants in, and then dove through the window with Zebra and Crawfish pulling on his arms. I popped the clutch with Squid's butt and legs hanging out the window, and Zebra and Crawfish holding on to him for dear life. We thundered out of there in a cloud of dust, right through the subdivision that was well lighted with street lamps. Squid's naked butt and legs were still hanging out the window. A lady standing by her mailbox laughed herself silly as we roared past her.

"Don't worry," I said, "there isn't a cop car in the county that can catch us." Crawfish and Zebra were able to eventually pull Squid into the car. Poor Squid was hurting.

"Damn, that yard. It is full of sandspurs. I must have a thousand stuck in my feet." moaned Squid.

"Shit," I said, "don't get those things all over the inside of the car. Wait a few minutes and I'll stop somewhere and we'll help pull them out." Once I thought we were out of harm's way, we stopped. Squid was right. He must have had a thousand burs stuck in the bottom of his feet, because it took us a while to pick them all out. His feet were bleeding, he lost his shirt, socks, tennis shoes, and under drawers, and to top it off he didn't get laid. At least he had his pants, wallet and car keys. We stopped as soon as possible and bought Squid a new pair of hush puppies. He had a shirt, socks and under drawers in his duffel bag, which was in my trunk, because he had checked out for the weekend to stay at our house.

It was still too early in the evening to call it a day, and we were in a mischievous mood. Being that it was Friday, we knew that there would be a crowd at AJ's Place, a drive-in restaurant across the street from Andrew Jackson High School. AJ's was a hang-out for Jackson students. I had some thoughts on how to cause a little calamity at AJ's. The other guys liked my ideas, and hardly anybody knew us on the north side, so we went into action.

I pulled a lever on the floorboard that tipped my license plate down in the rear, so it couldn't be read. Then I removed my .357 magnum and several blank cartridges from the glove compartment. Our plan was to raise a ruckus in AJ's parking lot and after getting everybody's attention we would jump out of the car and shoot Zebra several times.

"Deano, are you sure that those bullets are blanks?" inquired Zebra.

"Of course!"

"I mean, are you absolutely positive that they are blanks?"

"Zebra, if they aren't, I'll tell the judge that I was certain they were. He will let me off with manslaughter."

"Damn Deano!"

"Don't sweat it Zebra. You will be fine."

Zebra got out of the car a half-block away, and walked into the restaurant parking lot. He began talking with one of the curb girls who was waiting on customers. I squealed into AJ's and slammed on the brakes in the middle of the lot, in order to create as much attention as I could. Squid, Crawfish and I all jumped out of the car yelling at Zebra. I pulled out my pistol and shot Zebra three times right in front of a crowd of onlookers, and the horrified waitress he was talking with. Zebra doubled up, grabbing his gut, and then he collapsed on the pavement. Squid and Crawfish picked up Zebra, as I quickly opened the trunk. They stuffed him in, and slammed the lid. We leaped back into the car and burned rubber as we left AJ's parking lot. After rounding two or three corners, I stopped to let Zebra out of the trunk. He was holding his head.

"Shit," said Zebra. "When you peeled out of AJ's you

slammed me against the trunk lid. I can feel a lump popping up already."

"Sorry," I said. I thought you would be okay. Sorry."

We waited about ten minutes, then drove back past AJ's. There were three police cars sitting in the parking lot with their red lights flashing. We laughed and drove on.

After dropping Crawfish and Zebra at Kane, Squid and I headed to my house. Carrie and Sharon were there. The folks had gone to their bridge club, and Tina was out for night, so we had the house to ourselves. I wasn't sure whether, or not, Sharon had told Carrie about the Green Beacon, so I didn't mention it. We told the girls about the shooting at AJ's, however, and they both thought it was hilarious. About one hour after we arrived at the house, the doorbell rang. Carrie opened the door. Two inquisitive policemen began asking her questions about the Plymouth in the driveway. I was glad we had told her about AJ's, because she handled matters just fine.

"Ma'am, we had a report that a car resembling the black Plymouth in your driveway was possibly involved in a shooting on the north side earlier tonight."

"Really?" said Carrie. "Well, that car belongs to my father. He and my mother have been at their bridge club all evening. They took his Kaiser Darrin, and his Plymouth has just been sitting in our driveway." Carrie knew that the Plymouth was titled in Dad's name, in case they checked.

"Okay," said the officer. "We wanted to check it out. Thanks for filling us in."

I peeked out the window to see one of the officers placing his hand on the hood of the car, presumably to see if it was warm. After the policemen left, I gave Carrie a hug. Something I didn't do very often.

Sharon, Carrie, Squid and I spent all day and all evening together on Saturday. We went horseback riding, skeet shooting, and installed new carpet in the cabin of the Chris-Craft. Then we changed clothes and had dinner at the country club, because Mom had given Susan the day off.

My relationship with Sharon is stronger than ever. As for Carrie and Squid, they are constantly thrown together, and are good friends, but there is no romantic interaction.

CHAPTER THIRTY-THREE

The Blue Sail

Sunday afternoon, I dropped Squid off at KMA so he could check in, and then headed to the Blue Sail Motel at Jacksonville Beach where they were holding a reservation for me.

I put a note under the windshield wiper of my car indicating what room I was in. Miss Mary Ann showed up at about 4 p.m., read the note and knocked on the door. When I opened the door, she laughed.

"What's so humorous?" I asked.

"Oh, I don't know. It just struck me funny that it has always been me that has opened the door for you, and I have always been in various stages of undress. Now you open the door for me, and you are fully dressed." she said, as she came in. "For some reason, I find it amusing."

"Well, if you want me to, I will step outside, give you three minutes to prepare yourself, then I'll knock on the door, and you can open it in whatever state of undress you wish to be in."

"I like that idea," she said, "three minutes is all I need."

Three minutes passed and I knocked on the door. I voice from inside hollered, "Come in the door is open."

There she was, lying on the bed, without a stitch on. One knee was bent, and her legs were slightly parted. Miss Mary Ann looked so inviting. I shed my clothing in a flash and dove on top of her. We had furious and passionate sex for the longest time. When I looked at the clock on the end table, it read 7:15 p.m. We had been at it for over three hours. I took her by the hand and led her to the shower. We climbed in together, soaped each other's bodies, rinsed off, got dressed, and then walked on the beach.

I gave Miss Mary Ann a more detailed explanation of exactly what Major Harden had told me during the meeting at his office. I told her that he had a list of five names, and that mine was one of them. Curiosity had gotten the best of me, so I came right to the point.

"Miss Mary Ann, were you having sex with five different cadets at the same time?" I asked.

"Corporal Bass, you are my favorite cadet, without question." She sidestepped my question, but she didn't need to answer it. Her reply was all the answer I needed.

I changed the subject. "Miss Mary Ann, one of my best friends has moved into the building next to you, Brad Marin and his wife."

"Yes, Brad was in my junior English class last year. I ran into him in the apartment office the other day and he told me that he was living there. I also heard that you were the best man at his wedding."

"Yes ma'am! I am hesitant to visit him because I don't want someone to see my car so near your apartment," I said.

"Maybe that's a good thing, Corporal Bass." she said. "You could visit me and always use the excuse that you were at Sergeant Marin's apartment."

I changed the subject again. "Occasionally, Corporal Brennan and I have discussed the hemline on your skirts." As I said that she grinned. "We are convinced that you raise your hemline slightly with each passing month. You can tell me anything, you know. Is that true? Do you really raise it?"

"Corporal Bass, you and Corporal Brennan are very observant. I have always liked to wear my skirts quite short. It often raises eyebrows with older people who are not accustomed to seeing a woman with a short skirt, and I know people talk. When I started working at Kane Military Academy in September of 1954, I was concerned that school management would frown upon it so I went out and bought several new, longer skirts. As time has passed I have shortened all of my skirts. You and Corporal Brennan are correct. My hemline continues to climb. Now, don't get me wrong. I am not raising it to excite the cadets. I do admit that I get a little rush when you, or any of the cadets, stare at my legs. But that is not the reason I raise my hemline."

"How much further do you intend to raise it?" I asked inquisitively, with a smile.

"How high do you think I can go without getting into trouble?" she asked, with a grin.

"I have no idea, but I like your skirts short." We both laughed at our conversation, as we continued to walk down the beach.

"Aren't you hungry?" she asked. "Let's go get something to eat."

"Now that you mention it, I am hungry. You have had me so occupied that I forgot all about eating."

I drove Miss Mary Ann to the Sea Turtle, a seafood restaurant in Atlantic Beach, just a few miles north of our motel. Dinner was great, and the company was also.

After we left the Sea Turtle, we drove back to the Blue Sail Motel, left a wake up call, got naked, jumped back into bed, and made whoopee one more time. I woke up in the morning with a nipple in my mouth, and wondered if it had been there all night long. Miss Mary Ann and I jumped in the shower together again, after dressing we checked out and departed in our own vehicles for Kane Military Academy.

As I drove back into Jacksonville, different thoughts crossed my mind. Being cuddled up all night long with a soft, gorgeous woman was something that definitely appealed to me. On the other hand, I had about convinced myself that I probably should quit fooling around with Miss Mary Ann. She, I was certain, should be categorized as a nymphomaniac.

CHAPTER THIRTY-FOUR

A Predicament

When I arrived at Franklin Hall, Squid was still in the room. "Sit down Deano, I've got some bad news for you."

"What?" I asked. "Did somebody die."

"Just as bad," said Squid. "Sharon knows about you and Miss Boobs."

My heart sank. "How in hell could she? What makes you think so?"

"Carrie called me last night. Actually, Sharon tried to call you first. She was informed that you were checked out."

"Wait a minute. Back up. Start at the beginning. Are you sure she knows?"

"Here's what I know," said Squid. "Artie Mann was freaking out because he is on a list that Major Harden has of cadets that have been visiting Miss Boobs' apartment. He saw the list, and saw your name on it."

"New boy Artie Mann, that we marched through horse shit?"

"Yeah!"

"I'm going to kill that son-of-a-bitch."

"No, you don't understand," said Squid. "He didn't mean any harm. Artie and Sharon are cousins. He didn't know that she was dating you."

"Are you telling me that my Sharon and Artie Mann are cousins?"

"Evidently they are second cousins. Sharon ran into Artie yesterday afternoon. They sat and talked about a number of things, before the conversation settled on Kane Military Academy. He told her that he had been fooling around with a female instructor here at school, but that he had been caught, and that he was afraid he would be expelled. He told her that the instructor had been banging four other cadets as well, and that he saw a list of names of who they were. Supposedly, Sharon said she knew a few cadets and coerced the names from him. It wasn't until after Artie mentioned your name that Sharon told him that she was dating you. Artie asked her not to say anything to you, but she told him she had to confront you with it. Sharon called Carrie and told her the whole story. Then she tried to call you, only to find out that you were checked out. She probably assumes that you were with 'the female instructor'."

"Shit, shit, shit!"

"So, Sharon called Carrie back, and Carrie called me," said Squid.

"What did you tell Carrie?"

"Only that I had no clue where you were. Nor did I know anything about anything."

"Shit Squid, that made it worse. Carrie knows that you would obviously be aware of wherever I might be."

"Carrie is not going to say anything that would incriminate you, even if she knew something."

"I am going to kick Artie's ass."

"That wouldn't be very bright Deano. It certainly wouldn't get you any points with Sharon."

"You're right, Squid. You are absolutely right."

"Don't do anything foolish."

"The girls are probably on their way to Lee High by now. I guess I will try to call them late this afternoon. Meanwhile, I know where I can find Artie at the mess hall during lunch."

"I'm sorry, to give you such shitty news this morning."

"Earlier, when Major Harden called me down to his office, to confront me with this matter, I was under the impression that the school brass was just suspicious. But it sounds to me like somebody actually caught Artie with Miss Mary Ann. Maybe Hardass just didn't want to tell me the whole story. But that doesn't make sense either. If she had been caught having sex with any cadet, she would have been terminated. It could be that Artie Mann overreacted, or that Hardass scared the shit out of him. It doesn't sound to me like anybody has any proof of anything."

"You'll know more when you talk to Artie."

"What in the hell am I going to tell Sharon. I don't want to lie to her. But damn, I better not tell her the whole truth either. I need a beer."

"It's too early in the morning. We better get to class."

I didn't learn a thing in class this morning. My mind has been totally on what I was going to say to Sharon. Fourth period English is our last class before lunch. When the bell rang to dismiss the class, I lingered behind in order to speak briefly with Miss Mary Ann. "What happened between you and Artie Mann," I asked.

"I'm sure you know what happened, Corporal Bass," she uttered.

"Were you two caught, or what?"

"No, what makes you think that?"

"I don't know. Maybe Artie just has a big mouth. I'll find out."

"The Blue Sail was wonderful. I had a very enjoyable time."

"I did too," I added, as I walked out of the classroom.

I walked over to Artie Mann's table during mess and asked him to meet me in the outside corridor after lunch. He said he would.

I waited, and he finally approached. "Recruit Mann, the next time you fetch a bucket of horseshit, I am going to stick your head right in it. Do you understand?"

"Corporal Bass, I am so sorry. I should never have mentioned your name to my cousin. I had no idea that you two were dating. I had no idea that she even knew you. I really apologize."

"Look, why were you freaking out about this whole thing? Did you get caught with Miss Mary Ann or what?"

"I assume that somebody saw me coming out of her apartment. Major Harden asked me how many times I visited her."

"How many did you?"

"Seven, I think."

Shit, I thought, that was more than I did. "What did you tell Major Harden that you were doing over there?"

"Studying Shakespeare."

"Sharon never told me that she had a cousin here at Kane."

"She didn't know. I hadn't seen her since last summer. She didn't know that I had enrolled here."

"Why did you tell Sharon that you had been caught and were concerned that you might get expelled?"

"Well, I was caught. I mean I wasn't caught at her place, but if I hadn't been caught I wouldn't be on Major Harden's list. And, my dad will slaughter me if I get expelled."

"Artie Mann, you are one dumb fuck. Furthermore, you have put me in a seriously shitty predicament with my girlfriend."

"I'll talk to Sharon and straighten things out for you."

"Lord no, don't even say another word to her. You will just screw things up worse."

"All right, I won't. I'm sorry that I caused you a problem."

"If I am fortunate enough to walk down the aisle with Sharon one day, I will be unfortunate enough to gain one really stupid ass, dumb fuck for a cousin-in-law."

Artie Mann bowed his head and walked off.

I can't believe this, I thought. The same guy that we recruited to get the horse shit, and one of the guys that marched through it, turns out to be Sharon's cousin. To top it off, he's fornicating Miss Boobs, and now he has screwed me up with Sharon. I am probably dead.

I was definitely down in the dumps. After drill, I went to the smoking lounge, dropped a coin in the juke box and played *Heartbreak Hotel*. I plopped down in an easy chair and just sat there thinking about my predicament.

CHAPTER THIRTY-FIVE

Dead or Alive?

I didn't want to lie to Sharon, because if she ever found out that I lied to her she would never trust me again. On the other hand, I knew that I couldn't tell her the whole unabridged blow-by-blow scenario or it just might make matters worse. It was a matter of life or death.

By a stroke of luck, Bones Gifford was absent from drill Monday afternoon, so my friend Brad was in charge. I told Brad to please cover for me, because I had to go A.W.O.L. for about an hour.

"Everyone will notice your car leaving the premises. Here take mine." Brad tossed me his keys.

"Thanks good buddy." I cranked up Brad's Chevy and headed to the nearest florist. It was located in the shops at Lakewood. I ordered four dozen red roses to be delivered to Sharon at four p.m. sharp. I signed the card, 'To the most fantastic girl in the galaxy, with extraordinary love, Dean.' I hoped with all my heart that the roses might soften whatever I would tell her later on this evening. I hightailed it back to school, and thanked Brad again.

I was able to get one of the pay phones at 5 o'clock. I knew I couldn't say all the things I wanted to because there is always a crowd around the bank of telephones. Needless to say, I was as nervous as a chicken in a fox den. I dialed. It pleased me that Sharon answered the call.

"Hi," I said.

"Hi."

"I love you so very much."

"Usually when a guy sends his girl this many flowers it is because he is begging her forgiveness for something that he believes would break her heart."

"You are very astute."

"Continue. Tell me your version of what happened."

"I will not lie to you. I will not deceive you by distorting what actually happened. You mean way too much to me. All I ask is that you hear me through, for better, or for worse. I need to talk in a low voice so half the world doesn't hear what I have to say. There are a lot of guys around these phones. This is something I would feel better about if I could talk to you in person, but I know you need an explanation now. Not when I see you. So, here goes. Miss Mary Ann Tolliver is an English teacher at Kane. She is stacked and very pretty. Not as pretty as you, but pretty. All of the cadets, and I mean all of the cadets, get weak knees when they talk to her. She is the most talked about person on campus. Miss Mary Ann wears her skirts quite high, and seems to thrive on all of the attention she gets. She is, I am sure, a nymphomaniac. I don't know how many cadets she has had sex with. Most of the cadets call her Miss Boobs. Not to her face, of course. She invites students over to her apartment to help her move furniture, listen to recordings of Shakespeare, or for other reasons. For a guy in high school, it is sort of like going to a whore house. It was for sex, and for no other reason. Artie and I both were caught in the trap, so to speak. I first went to her apartment long before you and I were dating. Artie told you about the list. Major Harden has a list of names of five cadets, that the school brass knows have visited Miss Mary Ann. Artie and I are both on the list. Lord knows how many students have been there that they don't know about. I was wrong to have ever gone over to her apartment in the first place. She asked me to help her move some furniture, and that is the reason I went. I spoke with Artie after lunch today. He admits that he wasn't really "caught," and that he overreacted in the way he presented the story to you. He also suggested to me that he talk with you again to help straighten things out. I told him no, that he had already done enough damage. Yes, like Artie, and probably like a lot of guys, I have had sex with Miss Mary Ann. I was wrong, and I was stupid. It will not ever happen again, with her or anybody else as long as we are going with each other. Will you please forgive me?"

"Dean, you have never indicated that we were going together, even though I assumed so. If we haven't been going together, I have no say so as to what you may or may not do. I am not saying that I'm not hurt, but you mean so much to me that I'm inclined to forgive you. Why don't we just consider this matter "history." I knew that you weren't a virgin, and you knew that I wasn't before we started dating. That doesn't mean that we can't be faithful and true to each other from this day forth, that is, if you will ask me officially to go steady with you, and if I were to accept."

"I love you with all my heart. Will you, officially, go steady with me?"

"Only if you promise to be completely faithful and true to me."

"I promise. You will never have to be concerned about anything like this again."

"I believe you, and yes, I accept. Of course, I would have believed you if you had denied the whole thing with your English teacher."

"But then I wouldn't have told you the truth, and you would have wondered about it for the rest of your life."

"You're probably right!"

"I'm sure."

"Our whole house has a marvelous aroma of red roses. They are so beautiful. Thank you very much."

"You deserve it. Just a little token of my love for the most fantastic girl anywhere. Let's plan a trip somewhere, out of town. Just the two of us, alone."

"That sounds great. If our folks will let us go."

After we hung up, I put my forehead against the telephone momentarily, with great relief, and then spun around to see who was hanging over my shoulder.

"Did I hear you right? Did you have sex with Miss Boobs?"

I grabbed Moncrief by his uniform tie and slammed him up against the wall. "If you utter a single word of my private conversation to anybody, you will have to deal with me. Understand?"

"Don't worry Bass, I won't say anything."

I went back to our room and plopped down in my recliner. Squid was gone, so I just tilted back, deep in thought. Golly, Sharon made it so easy for me. It was like she excused me for being an asshole. She didn't even ask me where I was last night. I'm sure the thought crossed her mind. She probably didn't ask me because she didn't want to know. What have I done to deserve such a super girlfriend? I was certain after all this that I would be faithful and true to Sharon, without question. In no way was I ever again going to do anything to jeopardize this relationship. It means too much to me. I believe that this whole situation has made me love her even more.

CHAPTER THIRTY-SIX

Big Boom

Everybody calls me a prankster, but in actuality, I really don't pull too many. It is times like this week, at school, when I have a little pent-up energy, that I feel the necessity to liven things up a bit.

The fuse receptacle, that little hole in the top of a cannon through which a fuse is inserted, and through which a fuse burns, was welded closed on the cannon in Hard-ass Circle. It was probably done back when the place was originally a hotel, so that the cannon would not fire - they thought - therefore eliminating any potential danger that the weapon might pose. Welding that hole closed simply turned the cannon into a sort of statue, for people to look at. Nobody ever considered the possibility that it still might actually shoot - except me.

Firearms are one of my pet things. It doesn't matter what kind. Pistols, rifles, shotguns, or cannons. I started rounding up supplies: Ten feet of fuse, gunpowder, soap, and a plunger. Each of our bathrooms had a "plumber's friend," or plunger, but I didn't want to use ours. I talked Crawfish into getting me the one that was in Fulton Dames' old quarters. I removed the handle and replaced it with a long broom handle. Joey Tighe, our Coors delivery day boy, got a supply of gunpowder and a small roll of fuse for me on Wednesday. There are fast burning fuses and slow burning fuses. He bought the slowest that he could find. After taking a measurement of the inside diameter of the cannon barrel, I cut a little rubber off the plunger so it would match. Then I melted the soap on my illegal hot plate and fused it into a cylinder with the same diameter. I cut a groove down the length of the soap so the fuse could bypass it. Then I put a small knot in the end of the ten foot fuse, and encased it in putty. I was ready. The only people that knew what I was up to were Squid, Zebra, Crawfish, Tommy, who was Squid's old roommate, and Joey. The only way in, or out, from the third floor of Franklin Hall was either through the main entrance, or one of the fire escapes. There was always someone on duty at the main entrance, around the clock, so naturally I elected to leave and re-enter by way of the fire escape that was closest to my room. Squid was my watch dog.

It was 3 a.m. on Thursday morning when I crept down the fire escape and out to Hard-ass Circle. The campus was quiet, but there were plenty of lights on everywhere, so I had to be careful not to be seen. When I arrived at the cannon, I happened to notice Captain Bohanon's old car, with all the "I Like Ike" stickers plastered all over it, sitting way down the entrance drive. BoBo didn't live on campus, so it must have broken down to be parked where it was. If I had been shooting a cannonball, I thought, his car might be right in the trajectory, but I am only shooting soap. The gunpowder was in a large pouch with a drawstring. The end of the fuse that was encased in putty was inserted into the pouch. The fuse was also tied to the drawstring so it wouldn't pull loose. I inserted the pouch into the cannon barrel and pushed it all the way back with the plunger, which was my ramrod. The long fuse draped out the front of the barrel. This is like preparing a muzzle-loader, I thought. Then I shoved the cylinder of soap all the way back and packed it tight with the plunger. I pulled out my cigarette lighter, lit the fuse and dashed as fast as I could back to the fire escape. I bounded up the metal steps two and three at a time. When I reached the third floor I peeled the duct tape off the door latch that I had used to assure reentry. Then, I pulled off my tennis shoes and quietly raced down the hall to my room. "Did you see anybody out there, Squid?"

"Only you! Is it lit?"

"It's lit," I said, as I pulled off my tennies, jeans, and sweat shirt. My pj's were on underneath.

"Balooom," went the cannon. The reverberation was so strong that it rattled our third floor windows. The sound probably could have been heard for blocks. Lights came on all over Franklin Hall. Cadets looked out their windows. Some peered out into their hallway. We flipped our lights on, as well.

"I think I had too much gunpowder in that pouch," I whispered to Squid.

"Sure was loud," he indicated.

A spot inspection was called at 400 hours. We were all out in the hall, in our pajamas, at attention. Joseph Absalom spent a lot of time in our room. He picked up my tennis shoes and asked, "Who do these belong to?"

"They are mine, sir," I declared.

"Corporal Bass, get dressed and report to Major Harden's office immediately." Absalom said as he walked out of the room with my tennis shoes.

"Yes, sir."

Well, I thought that I had been very careful, but Absalom had found traces of gunpowder on my tennis shoes. I figured the best thing to do was admit it.

I put on fifteen pairs of undershorts and stuffed them with my sponge rubber pad, then went down to the major's office.

When I got to Major Harden's office, he said, "Come with me Corporal Bass!" I followed him outside, at 4:30 a.m. no less, across to Harden Circle. He stood looking at the cannon for the longest time. He bent over and sniffed the end of the cannon barrel. Then we walked down the entrance drive to Captain Bohanon's car. The windshield had been completely blown out, and there was soap everywhere. "Corporal Bass, would you explain to me just how you were able to fire the cannon, how you loaded it and why you had to damage Captain Bohanon's automobile."

"Sir, I had no intention of doing any damage. Not to Captain Bohanon's car or to anything else. The cannon was loaded with soap, as you can see. I thought that the soap would simply splatter against anything that it hit. Furthermore sir, I didn't think it would carry so far." I talked as fast as I could in my defense. We walked back to Harden Circle and he stood there again looking at the cannon. He must have liked the smell of gunpowder, because he leaned over and took another whiff. He then ordered me to follow him back to his office.

"Corporal Bass, I sentence you to Bull Ring, Saturday and Sunday, plus ten swats. Do you understand?"

"Yes, sir."

"You are a very clever lad, and I will not take away your rank, if you will show me how we can fix the cannon so nobody else will ever be able to fire it."

"Yes, sir. Thank you, sir. I can definitely show you how."

"Assume the position!" he said. That meant bend over and grab hold of my ankles, while I received ten swats with his fancy, thin paddle with all the holes drilled in it. I sure was glad that I anticipated the swats, and dressed accordingly. When I entered the smoking lounge later on everybody cheered and clapped. The word had spread like wildfire throughout Franklin Hall.

During fourth period English, every time Miss Mary Ann looked my way, she couldn't help but grin.

I told Major Harden that the way to fix the cannon so it couldn't be fired, was to block the whole barrel off. I suggested welding a cannonball, or steel plate, about 12 inches inside the opening. Maybe Hardass was giving me a break, I concluded. Any military guy should know how to block off that barrel.

Damn, I thought, after the situation with Sharon I was really hoping to see her this coming weekend. I guess I should have realized that there was a chance I might get caught, and subsequently confined. Once again, I was stupid. Well, hopefully the roses won't wilt for awhile, and will help to keep her thinking of me.

CHAPTER THIRTY-SEVEN

Nasty Nellie

I don't know who cleaned the soap from Captain Bohanon's old Hudson. I had to write a check to BoBo for $32.00 so he could replace his windshield. He wasn't the least bit upset. In fact, he actually seemed quite amused over the incident. He indicated that the windshield was cracked anyway, and that he needed a new one.

During study period Thursday evening, I let Squid in on a little secret.

"Squid, you are going to get laid later tonight, right here on the third floor of Franklin Hall, by a prostitute from the County Line."

"What?"

"I repeat, you are going to get laid tonight right down the hall from our room, in Fulton Dames' old quarters."

"What?"

"Your virginity is coming to a screeching halt sometime after 11 p.m. tonight."

"Are you shittin' me?"

"Nope!"

"How so?"

"Well, it's a long story. Your old roommate Tommy met this girl named Nellie at the Krystal last weekend. They sat and talked for a while as they ate their burgers. When she found out that he was a Kane cadet, she solicited him. He was able to convince her to sneak into the dorm tonight for a little gang bang. Tommy is going to let her in the fire escape door by Dames' apartment. Crawfish will have Dames' old quarters unlocked, and will take Nellie on first. As soon as he is done, Tommy will take over. Tommy will be followed by his brother, and then Zebra. Each of them will contribute ten bucks to the cause. You will be next, and your ten bucks will give her a total of fifty, good pay for an hours work."

"Are you shittin' me?

"Nope, it's all set. Nellie followed Tommy back to Franklin

Hall so he could show her where to park and what fire escape to take. They arranged the time and everything. It is all set for tonight, after everyone is asleep."

"She probably won't show up," said Squid.

"Tommy said she was excited about the idea of sneaking into a boy's dorm, and doing the do with a few. I believe she'll show up."

"How do you know she works at the County Line?'

"She told Tommy she did."

"I am going to ask her about those Doberman pinschers over there."

"Yeah, ask her."

"How long will it take the others to do their thing?"

"I have no clue."

"What time will I get to go to Dames' apartment?"

"When the others are through doing their thing."

"How come you're not getting in on this, Deano?"

"I'm just not."

"Well, I still have a condom in my glove compartment. I'll go get it after study hall. How long have you known about this and not told me?"

"Just a couple of days. I didn't want you to have an anxiety attack."

Everything went as scheduled. Nellie parked where Tommy had indicated, and she climbed the fire escape stairs to the third floor. Tommy was waiting with the door open at 11 p.m., and he escorted her quietly to Dames' old quarters. Crawfish invited her in, gave her ten bucks, and led the pack by being the first. It had been months since the apartment had been lived in, so the bed was stripped, and Nellie had to do it on a bare mattress. When Crawfish was through, he signaled Tommy, and he went next. Nellie collected ten from Tommy, and ten more from Tommy's brother. Squid waited patiently for his turn, with his condom in his hand. Zebra paid Nellie his ten, but before they were able to get it on, she excused herself to use the bathroom. According to Zebra, she was in there the longest time before and after the toilet flushed. Finally, she exited from the bathroom ahead of a river of water. "There is no plunger in there," she claimed, as she hurried to get dressed. She and Zebra both headed to the hall door in order to beat the flow of nasty stuff pouring from the commode. That nasty stuff ran out the front door and into the hall as Nellie dashed toward the fire escape and Zebra toward his room.

Nellie made a clean escape. Squid was left out in the cold again. Zebra lost ten bucks and didn't get laid. Crawfish couldn't lock up Dames' apartment because of all the crap in the hall. And, it was possibly all because I had used Dames' plunger for a ramrod when I fired the cannon in Hard-ass Circle. Nobody ever knew how Dames' door became open, or who used the commode in the apartment. Naturally, Major Harden asked, but nobody confessed.

CHAPTER THIRTY-EIGHT

Howard Hill Goes Berserk

Friday afternoon at the end of drill, something strange happened. One of the M-1 rifles disappeared. It was our practice to enter the armory single file. Each of us placed our rifle in the next available slot along the wall. After we had all gone through the armory, there was an empty slot, and nobody had a rifle. But, there was one missing from the armory. We were ordered back into formation. Major Harden arrived and he gave us a "that rifle had better turn up, or else" lecture. Nobody said a word.

I really shouldn't have felt too bad, because this was only my second weekend of Bull Ring this year. Both seemed to happen at the most inopportune time, however. By the same time last year, I had already been confined for four or five weekends slaving away at one duty or another.

After morning mess on Saturday, most everyone returned to their rooms, or went to the main lounge or smoking lounge which both faced the river. I dressed for Bull Ring in jeans, a tee shirt, and the tennis shoes that Major Harden gave back to me.

As I was preparing to start work outside of Franklin Hall, I heard a popping sound that sounded like firecrackers. I thought someone was shooting off fireworks. Suddenly some of the cadets came bolting out of the two lounges. Major Harden ran toward the main lounge. What is happening, I wondered. Somebody yelled, "There's a guy out there on the river shooting at the windows." I dashed up the tower stairs. There were several cadets in our room talking to Squid. Our room was the furthest from the river, and the guys were taking refuge. "What's happening?" I asked.

"Evidently, there is somebody sitting in a boat out on the river shooting at the building."
said one of the guys.

I scrambled down the tower stairs, and headed into the main lounge. Everyone was on the floor, including Major Harden and Joseph Absalom. "Get down he ordered!" I crawled over to the windows to take a look.

"Damn," I said, "it's that crazy Howard Hill. He's in the

Kane boat, and he's flying his Nazi flag. It looks like the anchor is down. I guess we now know where the missing M-1 is." All of a sudden, four policemen came running in with their guns drawn.

"Get down, and put those guns away," shouted Harden. "There will be no killing around here."

"We need to take that guy out before he kills somebody," snapped one of the cops, with his pistol still drawn.

Major Harden repeated his order, "Put your guns away!"

"That boat is out of range for your pistols, anyway," I said.

One of the cops looked at me and said, "I know you. You shoot with us at the police pistol range." Major Harden looked surprised.

"I do, and I know firearms. That boat is out of range for your .357's."

About that time several more shots came through the lounge windows.

"Major, I was just upstairs, and he is shooting out windows everywhere."

The nurse from our infirmary came in to see if anyone was hurt. Major Harden asked her to check the second and third floors, but to stay away from the windows, and she departed.

"I have an idea, sir," I said. "The M-1 takes .30-06 shells. I have two boxes of .30-06 shells in the trunk of my car, because I was teaching Corporal Brennan how to shoot. Please unlock the armory, sir, and bring me one of the rifles."

"Hell no Bass, you are not going to shoot Howard Hill."

"No sir, I wouldn't do that. I'll sink the boat, and he will have to swim ashore. He won't be able to swim with a rifle. Once the boat sinks, it will be safe to go down to the bank and get Hill."

"That's a good idea, sir," said the cop that knew me. "The boy can shoot!"

"What makes you so sure you can sink the boat, without hitting Cadet Hill?" asked Major Harden.

"I know I can, sir. Please get me a rifle."

"Bass, I can't authorize that. No sir! I just can't give you a rifle. Sinking the boat sounds like a viable solution, but I can't give you a rifle."

A few more shots came through the windows of the main

lounge. I motioned to Joseph Absalom and the cop that knew me, to follow me outside, and they did. Absalom always unlocked the armory door prior to drill period, so I knew he had a key.

"Joseph, we need to get a rifle out of the armory and end this matter before Hill kills somebody." I said. "Get one and give it to this officer, and I will show him where there is a good vantage point from which to shoot. I'll get my .30-06 shells out of my car, if you'll get a rifle."

"I think that's a good idea," said the cop.

"Deano, I'll get a rifle and give it to the officer, not to you. Don't take it near the lounges or the major will raise hell."

"I will take the officer down to the boathouse," I said.

I dashed to my car and got the shells, then headed toward the armory. Joseph had pulled an M-1 from one of the racks and had given it to the patrolman.

"For Christ's sake be careful." said Absalom. "I will go back into the lounge and tell Major Harden that I got a rifle out for one of the policemen, and hope that he doesn't kick my ass."

The officer and I ran around the south end of the building. I hope somebody has sighted this rifle in recently, I thought.

We got to the boathouse without Hill seeing us. The cop handed me the rifle and I opened a box of shells and loaded it. I didn't offer it back to the officer. I crouched by the nearest corner of the boathouse, steadying the M-1 by resting my left arm on a cut off piling. I slowly squeezed the trigger, and drilled the aft end of the boat, just below the waterline. Then I shot again, with the same result. After the third shot, Howard Hill dove out of sight. Not knowing where he was, within the confines of the hull, I didn't dare shoot. I remembered Hill saying, 'I love boats. When I die I want to be buried in a boat.' Meanwhile, one of the cops was yelling at Hill on a megaphone, from up at the main lounge, trying to convince him to give up. I kept my sight on the rear end of the boat. When I saw Hill's head pop up near the bow, I fired again, and then again. I was hoping that I could get that old boat to take on some water.

The thought crossed my mind that this is almost like war. Here I was with an M-1, shooting at a boat flying a Nazi flag.

For the most part, Hill stayed down. I believe he thought

that I was shooting at him. Finally, the boat began to list just a little, then a little more. Hill stayed out of sight. I thought about shooting his Nazi flag, but didn't. It was a slow process, but it was working. The boat took on more, and more, water. Eventually, it rolled over on its side. Howard Hill was hanging on to a life preserver. As long as any part of the boat was afloat, he stayed out there with it. Finally it completely capsized, and all that could be seen was a bit of the hull. With the "donut" around him, and no rifle in sight, Howard Hill swam to shore to be greeted by several policemen who immediately clamped handcuffs on him.

That was the last time I ever saw Cadet Hill. We later learned that he was sentenced to two years in a reformatory.

Major Harden had watched the whole ordeal from a lounge window. When it was over, he approached me and said, "Corporal Bass, you are dismissed from Bull Ring. And, thank you!" I ejected my other shells, put them back in the box, handed Major Harden the M-1, and reminded him, with a grin, that the rifle needed cleaning before it was put away. I changed clothes, and then checked out for the rest of the weekend so I could spend some much needed time with Sharon.

CHAPTER THIRTY-NINE

Savannah

One of the best St. Patrick's Day parades in the country occurs in Savannah, Georgia, just a half day drive up U.S. Highway 17 from Jacksonville. Sharon and I each began a campaign to get our folks to allow us to go to Savannah together, unchaperoned, for the weekend. St. Pat's Day fell on a Saturday. So, March 17th, was destined to be an extra popular one. Actually, Savannah was just an excuse for us to go somewhere. We didn't really care where we went, just as long as we could go. By now, I felt certain, that Sharon's folks and my folks all realized that we were having sex anyway, so it shouldn't matter to them if we traveled somewhere together. Sharon indicated that her parents wanted to talk to me about it.

I questioned Sharon, "What should I say if they come right out and ask me if we are having sex?"

"Tell them that we are."

"Are you sure?"

"I think they probably know anyway," she said.

"But, there's a difference between assuming we are, and knowing for sure."

"Look at it this way, if they are sure we are, they will be more apt to let us go off by ourselves. Don't you think so?"

"I have no idea. When I asked my folks, Dad said, 'Let me think about it,' so I have no clue what they think either. If I was going somewhere with some guys, I wouldn't need to ask"

"Oh well, if they won't let us go, we can always check into a motel all day." Sharon said.

"It's not the same. It's not like spending the night to-gether."

"How do you know? Have you ever slept with a girl, like all night long?"

"No." I lied. Even though I told Sharon that I wouldn't lie to her, I did.

"Well okay, then you're not an authority. I guess we'll just have to wait and see what they all say." said Sharon.

We went to Sharon's house so we could talk with her parents. They didn't say anything about sex. "Dean," said Sharon's father, "we have heard through the grapevine that you have a very fast car, and furthermore, that you drive it with a heavy foot."

"Sir, I do have a fast car, but I don't drive it fast when Sharon, or anybody else, is riding with me." I lied again. "I have raced at the Thunderbolt Dragway, but Sharon was not in the car." That time I told the truth.

"You know, if I ever find out that you are speeding with my daughter in your car, she will not ride with you again. I like you, Dean, but I don't want Sharon's life endangered. I hope you understand that I am a concerned parent. I also hope you understand that I mean what I say."

"Sir, I would never do anything to endanger Sharon, in any way, and, yes I understand."

"Dean, if it is all right with your parents, and I have your promise to drive within the speed limit, the two of you may go to Savannah."

"Thank you, sir, you have my promise. Please don't worry, she is in good hands."

With half of the mule skinned, we drove over to my house to talk with Dad and Mom. They were in the den reading the newspaper. When I asked him if he had thought it over, his reply was, "Sure, I don't see anything wrong with you going. Just be careful, be smart, and have a nice time."

Sharon and I walked out of the den on cloud nine. To Sharon, I said, "That was easy."

It was Friday, March 16th. We had originally planned to leave Jacksonville late in the afternoon. For a number of reasons, we were delayed, and didn't get out of town until after 10 p.m. I had planned to gas up before we left town, and figured I could stop at a station on the north side. As we headed up Highway 17, there were absolutely no stations open. The gauge registered about one-third. I told Sharon that we needed to gas up within the hour, or we would run out. We crossed the state line into Georgia, and still no stations open. Eventually, the engine sputtered, and I pulled over on the shoulder of the road. There was no traffic on the highway. We had a motel reservation in Savannah, and they were expecting us late, so we weren't too worried about that, but it was already past midnight, and we were out in the boondocks.

We sat there wondering what we should do, when I spotted truck headlights in the rear view mirror. I got out of the car and flagged the truck driver down. He stopped. I couldn't believe it. It was a gasoline tanker. The driver informed me that there was a $10,000 fine for pumping gasoline from a tanker directly into another motor vehicle and he wasn't going to jeopardize his job. He indicated, however, that he could pump gas into a gas can, or most any kind of container. I told him that I didn't have a gas can, or any kind of container.

As the three of us walked up and down along the ditch adjacent to the highway looking for something, just anything to put some gas in, another set of truck headlights approached in the distance. I walked out to the edge of the highway, and flagged the driver down. He also stopped. It was a flatbed. The only thing on the back of his truck was an empty 15 gallon gas can chained to the bed. The driver of the tanker filled the gas can to the top. Two of us tipped it up and poured it into my car. Neither of the drivers would take a cent for the gas, or the help. I put a squirt in the top of the carburetor to assure quick ignition, and fired it up. The gas gauge jumped to three-quarters, and it was free. Our luck was fantastic. I told Sharon that it was probably an omen that we were going to have a great weekend.

We checked into our motel about 1:30 a.m. People were out partying, but we were a little too tired to join them. It certainly wasn't too late to make love though, so we did, and then cuddled the rest of the night.

I woke up Saturday morning with a smile on my face, thinking, that was much better than the night I recently spent with Miss Mary Ann. I needed to stop seeing that nympho, and I needed to back off the sex with Tina, and give Sharon my undivided attention. I tried to convince myself that my will power could handle it.

Sharon opened her eyes, and said, "I love you!"

"And, I love you!" I declared.

"Happy St. Patrick's Day!" she stated.

"And a happy one to you too," I said, as we both smiled.

We showered together, and then departed for breakfast. Sharon and I each ate a stack of pancakes before we drove to the parade route. The St. Patrick's Day parade was great. Individuals were clad in kelly green, riding on floats that were also clad in kelly green. It never occurred to us to pack any green clothes, but somebody gave us two green carnations, so we were at least wearing something green. As we watched, a nun twisted her ankle and bumped into a man standing near us. She apologized and moved on. At the time we thought nothing of it. I suggested to Sharon that we move down about a half block to see if we could improve our vantage point, so we did. We hadn't been at our new location but just a few minutes, when the same nun reappeared and stumbled again, this time into another man. "That sure is a clumsy nun," I said.

"Bless her heart," added Sharon. "She keeps bumping into people."

The nun quickly departed, moving along behind the crowd. The man who had been bumped must have sensed that some-thing was wrong. He patted his butt, and then hollered, "I've been robbed! Someone stole my wallet."

Our minds flashed back to the first incident we witnessed of the nun bumping into the other man. We immediately told the second man about the first incident, and that we thought the nun might be the thief. Sharon hailed a policeman who was walking along the parade route beside some Shriners on their motor scooters. He hailed some other patrolmen on his walkie-talkie. Sharon explained to the first officer what had happened, as we headed in the direction that we saw the nun take. About a block away, we spotted her. As we got close, we could see that she was approaching a mail box with a brown paper bag that had a label affixed to it. The officer ran to the mail box and grabbed her bag before she could stuff it in the box. Other officers arrived on the scene and the nun couldn't run. The first officer read the label: Mary Louise Harper, 5555 Bridgewater Road, Atlanta, Georgia.

"Let me guess," he stated, "You are Mary Louise Harper, and you are mailing this bag to yourself. Am I right?"

"Sister Mary Louise, sir."

"Sister, why would you be mailing this bag to yourself?"

"I just didn't want to carry the items around while I was here in Savannah." She said

"Well, said the officer let's open the bag and see what's inside."

"You can't do that," she insisted. "That would be tampering with United States mail, which is a federal offense."

"Sorry ma'am, this bag hasn't been mailed yet." As he spoke he ripped the bag open and four wallets fell out. "Sister Mary Louise, you are under arrest." The officer thanked us for being so observant. After putting the nun into the back seat of his patrol car, he gave us a statement to sign, which we both did, before heading back to watch the parade. The festivities lasted nearly two hours, altogether. We found out later that Mary Louise was no nun, but a pickpocket with a record of many arrests.

Later that afternoon, there was some partying going on at some of the bars on Broughton Street and Bay Street. I had a fake ID, but when I tried to get Sharon into a couple of bars, they wouldn't admit her. So, we put two six-packs of Schlitz in our cooler and drove to the beach at Tybee Island. That evening we changed clothes and went to the Pirate's House for dinner. The Pirate's House actually was once a pirate's house, bar, and brothel. It opened as a restaurant in 1948, and quickly became very popular. Sharon had lobster and I had steak.

We sat across from each other during dinner. "You should be in movies," I said. "Your gorgeous green eyes and colossal figure are matched only by your radiant personality."

Sharon laughed, and said, "only? What about my intelligence? Does it not match up?"

"Absolutely, it does, as does your beautiful hair, tasteful wardrobe, exceptional common sense, incredible perception, and amazing compassion and consideration. You are perfection in a woman. Everywhere you go you turn heads. Everybody looks at you."

"Keep going!" she said with a grin.

"I love you so much," I added.

"Dean Bass, you are truly the best thing that has ever happened to me. I hope we will be together the rest of our lives. I love you with all my heart."

After dinner we went back to the motel to polish off the rest of our beer, and make love for half of the night.

Sunday, we checked out early at our motel. I chartered a boat and took Sharon to see two of the South Carolina out islands nearby. We hit the road back to Florida about noon, and gobbled a couple of barbecue sandwiches in Brunswick on the way.

Shortly after crossing the Florida state line, we saw a work detail of prisoners ahead on the left. They were all dressed in their convict blues with white stripes down the side of their pants. It reminded me somewhat of our Kane uniforms, though ours are grey with black stripes.

"Look at those poor guys," said Sharon. "They look miserable. Is that a chain gang?"

"No, they got rid of chain gangs a few years ago." I slowed down as we eased past them. "Check out those armed guards with shotguns."

"That is so pitiful," exclaimed Sharon. "They are all so sweaty, and having to work on Sunday afternoon. It seems so unjust."

"I agree!"

"We should go buy them all ice-cold soda pops. There is a country store that we passed just a mile, or so, back up the road. Can we turn around and do it?" she asked.

"Sure, but we better get permission from one of the guards." I made a u-turn, and headed back. As we slowed down by the work detail, one of the guards waved his shotgun barrel in a motion for us to keep moving. Sharon rolled her window down and stuck her head out. When the guard saw how pretty she was, he stopped waving his shotgun, and I pulled up beside the guard. A couple of prisoners let out wolf whistles.

Sharon called out, "You all look so blistering hot. Would you mind if we bought you guys some cold drinks?"

"We have water coolers on the back of our bus, ma'am."

"But that's not like having an ice-cold RC Cola, Sir."

"That does sound tempting," stated the guard. "There are 14 of us all together, and if you really want to do that we would certainly appreciate it."

"We are glad to do it, and we'll be back shortly," said Sharon.

It took about 15 minutes for us to make the round trip to the store, and get back to the work detail. The guards must have said something to the prisoners while we were gone, because upon our return there was no more whistling. The men were very gracious and made comments like "thank you very much," and "y'all are good folks." We headed on down the road feeling very pleased about what we had just done.

"Dean, did you notice that only two of the prisoners were white? All of the rest were colored. Don't you think that more colored people are convicted by all-white juries, and that whites receive minor sentences, if any at all?"

"Yes, there is no doubt about it."

"It just doesn't seem fair," added Sharon.

Sharon and I were becoming very serious. My love for her was much deeper than it ever was for Linda. I had made up my mind to go to Jacksonville University during my freshman year in order to be close to Sharon. She and I discussed attending the University of Florida, in Gainesville, together the following year, which would be her freshman year. We were for the first time looking, with earnest, into the distant future.

CHAPTER FORTY

Billy's Bones?

Monday morning, I checked in at school before breakfast. There was a lot of commotion. Police cars, a couple of strange looking station wagons, a truck, and Health Department vehicles were parked all around Hard-ass Circle. I spotted Crawfish crossing the circle, and flagged him down.

"What's going on around here?" I asked.

"Oh man, the guys on Bull Ring yesterday discovered a skeleton tangled up in some branches that they pulled out of the river. Evidently, it was a young man. Everybody seems to think that it is the remains of Wilhelm von Kreisler. Major Harden indicated that Billy's father is flying here this afternoon to look at the bones, which are now at the morgue."

"Poor Billy," I said. I went to breakfast, and then had a little time before classes began, so I walked down to Major Harden's office. He was talking with Billy's roommate Carl. When he saw me, he motioned for me to come in. I saluted, and he returned my salute.

"Sir, I heard about the skeleton that the cadets on Bull Ring discovered yesterday, and that it might be Wilhelm."

"We are just assuming that it is," said Major Harden. "He is the only young man that has been reported missing, in this area, to the local authorities. The height of the remains seems to coincide with Wilhelm's height, about 5 ft. 10 inches. There were no fragments of clothing or anything else on the remains to help identify who it is, or was. Wilhelm's father, who is flying here this afternoon, is going to contact the office of their dentist in Germany so that dental records can be dispatched to the coroner's office here. That is all we know as of now. You may check back with me later, Corporal Bass, and I will pass along any new information that I might have."

"Thank you, sir!" I departed and headed to class. The skeleton was discussed in every class. Miss Mary Ann even had a tear in her eye when talking about it during 4th period.

That evening, during study period, Major Harden tapped

on our open door. "Corporals Bass and Brennan, there is a new development that I thought you might like to know about," he said. "Wilhelm's father arrived this afternoon, and went straight to the morgue. He could not identify his son after viewing the remains. Evidently, he studied the structure of the teeth for a long time before indicating that he couldn't tell if it was Wilhelm, or not. To complicate matters even more, he was told by friends in Germany that the dentist's office where both his and his son's records were located was destroyed by a bomb near the end of the war. He came by the school, looked at Wilhelm's old room, and talked with Cadet Carl and me for a while, then indicated that there was nothing else he could do here so he plans to fly back to Alabama tomorrow morning."

"Thanks for filling us in," I said, then added, "So, I guess there is a possibility that we will never know if the remains are those of Wilhelm, or not."

"Yes, that is a very distinct possibility," said Major Harden.

"What will happen to the skeleton, sir?"

"It will stay at the morgue for a while, as long as there is a chance it might be identified, and because they are still running tests on the remains.

The skeleton had been discovered so late Sunday afternoon that the story didn't make the Monday morning newspaper. When the story finally hit the streets, another twist to the story developed. Major Harden stayed abreast of developments, and continued to relay them on to us. Although local authorities had no other report of a missing young male person, federal authorities evidently did. A young seaman in the United States Navy, who was stationed at the Naval Air Station, across the river from Kane Military Academy, turned up missing several months earlier. For one reason or another, their missing persons alert went to all naval bases and the seaman's home state of Maryland, but not to Jacksonville, or Duval County authorities. When the newspaper article was called to the attention of certain concerned parties at NASJAX, they went through the same process in an effort to identify the remains. The seaman's parents flew to Jacksonville, but could not identify their son. When his dental records finally arrived from Maryland, they didn't match the teeth of the skeleton.

Meanwhile, Wilhelm's father called family members to advise them as to what had transpired. When he called his deceased wife's sister (Wilhelm's aunt), who despised Wilhelm's father, to tell her the story, she let out a hardy laugh. She told him that she had promised Wilhelm that she wouldn't tell where he was, because he didn't want his father to know, but she had to say something now. Now that everybody thought he was dead. She told him that Wilhelm had been living with her ever since he left school at Kane. Furthermore, he was back in classes at a high school near her house, and doing just fine.

Well, when Billy's father passed the news on to Major Harden, he told the whole school the story, and everyone was relieved. All of us got more than one laugh over the matter. I was glad to hear that Billy was alive and well.

As for the skeleton, it wasn't the seaman from the Naval Air Station. Maybe he will turn up somewhere unexpectedly as Billy did.

CHAPTER FORTY-ONE

Tina

The following Friday I checked out from school and spent most of the weekend hanging out with Sharon. We always enjoyed being together, regardless of what we were doing. Saturday morning, we walked around the Jacksonville Zoo, just holding hands and talking. We spent part of the afternoon walking on the beach at Little Talbot Island State Park. I took Sharon to her house so she could freshen up and change clothes, then we went to my house so I could do the same. She and I ate a marvelous dinner at the Timuquana Country Club before I drove her home.

It is amazing how love can alter your patterns of life. I had decided to be true blue, a real change for me. No more affairs with Miss Mary Ann, or Tina, or anybody else. Speaking of Tina, she and I were the only two people downstairs early Sunday morning, so naturally we engaged in an off-color conversation.

"I want your body, Dean Bass."

"Tina, you are fantastic, but I have decided to be faithful to Sharon. Things have gotten pretty heavy between us. I think we have a real future ahead of us, together."

"Dean, it is only sex. Our sex is good. Why should we stop something that we both seem to enjoy? Huh?"

"I just don't feel good about screwing around anymore. Please respect my wishes."

"Well, I work for your family, so I have no choice, but if you change your mind please let me be the first to know. Okay?"

"That's a deal!"

"I like Sharon," Tina said. "I wish you both all the luck in the world."

"Thanks! Now let me ask a huge favor of you."

"Ask!"

"Remember the conversation we had at the breakfast table a while back, about Squid being a virgin?"

"I do!"

"Well, the poor guy is still a virgin. Every time we think he is going to get laid, something goes awry. By now he must think he is going to go through life without any pussy."

"What are you saying," Tina asked. "Are you asking me to fuck him?"

"It's a thought. What do you think? Would you?"

Tina walked slowly around the kitchen. She was definitely contemplating the idea. Finally, she asked, "When?"

"How about this coming Thursday night? It's Easter weekend, so we get out a day early. The folks will be at a bridge party until late. It will be a perfect time. Susan will be gone by 7:00 p.m., so how about 8:00 o'clock? And just think, he will remember you the rest of his life because you were the first. Okay?"

Tina continued to walk slowly around the kitchen, in deep thought. "You're right, he would remember it the rest of his life. Everybody always remembers the first time. That might be nice. Yes, I'll do it."

"Blow his mind, like you did mine, with the see-through bikini, and so forth," I suggested.

"Leave it to me. I'll take care of him. "

"Thanks, Tina."

I was checked out from school until Monday Morning, so Sharon and I spent Sunday afternoon and evening together. I told her about my conversation with Tina, because I needed her help.

"Can you occupy Carrie for a while Thursday night? I need to get her out of the house, at least until late, like maybe 11:00 p.m. Can you do that? Squid likes Carrie a lot. He will not jump in the sack with Tina, if Carrie is in the house."

"I know how long you have been trying to help Squid lose his virginity, so I'll help in any way I can," she said. "Carrie will do whatever I ask. I'll come by and pick her up, then take her to my house for the evening."

"I'll miss you Thursday evening, but it's for a good cause. Thanks!"

I didn't get a chance to talk to Squid until study period on Monday. I convinced him to put down his *Dick Tracy* comic book and listen to me. I told him that I had great news for him. He was ecstatic.

"Are you kidding me?" he said. "She is a real beaver. Hell yes! Are you kidding me?"

If I had known that I would get that kind of reaction, I probably would have talked to Tina earlier about the possibility. Everything was set. Squid checked out with me Thursday. He followed me to the house in his car, so he could check back in at school Sunday night. When we arrived, Carrie had already gone with Sharon, but Dad, Mom, and Susan were still there. Mom gave me the bad news.

"Dean, in case you get any phone calls for the house-keeper job while we are gone, please take down their name and phone number so I can call them back tomorrow."

"Housekeeper job?" I asked. "What happened to Tina?"

"Well, I guess you wouldn't have heard, being at school all week. She called us from Las Vegas Monday night to inform us that she had gotten married, and was moving to Rochester, New York with her husband, whom she indicated was very old, but very rich. She said that it was a sudden decision, and she hated to quit without notice, but she had to do what she had to do. She asked us to put her belongings in a box and ship them to the address she gave me in Rochester, and I told her we would. I wished her good fortune, and asked her to send us a Christmas card to let us know how she was doing. She said she would."

Needless to say, Squid was certainly down in the dumps. He had been looking forward to seeing Tina all week. And, I couldn't believe it. I had just talked with Tina Sunday morning, and everything was set. Monday, the very next day, her day off, she is in Las Vegas, and married. Yes, I would say that was very sudden. Another bed-bouncer bites the dust, I thought. Maybe, just maybe it's for the best, however.

The evening was not totally lost. I called Sharon and told her what happened. She indicated that Carrie had not said a word about Tina quitting, or she would have tried to let me know. Anyhow, we decided that the four of us should go out, so Squid and I drove over to Sharon's house to pick them up. After ham-burgers at the Polar Bear Drive-In, we went to see *The Man with the Golden Arm* starring Frank Sinatra and Kim Novak. After the movie, we drove the girls back to Sharon's house because they had already both decided to spend the night there.

CHAPTER FORTY-TWO

April Fool?

Sharon brought Carrie back to our house the following morning in time for breakfast, and we hung out together all afternoon. Sharon planned to spend the night at our place. It was Friday night, March 30th, and there was a dance contest at the Neptune Club, at the beach. Carrie and I were pretty good at doing the Jersey bop. It had more acrobatic moves than the beach bop that most everybody was doing, so it attracted more attention. We had spent many hours around the house practicing to her 45 rpm rock n' roll records. The Neptune Club served liquor, but was notorious for allowing admission to those who were under age. We felt certain that they must have been paying off the sheriff. The club had a live brass band that was putting out some great sounds. They mixed slow dances with the jitterbug. The bop contest was the highlight of the night, so it wasn't scheduled until 11:00 p.m. Sharon and I had only danced together a few times, while Carrie and I had routines that we did extremely well, so Carrie and I signed up as a couple for the contest, while Sharon and Squid, who had never danced together, decided they would be spectators and just cheer us on.

When 11:00 p.m. rolled around, Carrie and I took our place out on the dance floor with the other contestants. According to the rules of the contest, each of the couples would continue dancing until tapped on the shoulder by one of the judges, which meant they were eliminated and should sit down. The last couple dancing was declared the winner. I don't think I ever saw Carrie dance so well. She followed all my moves to perfection. Tuck toe, heel over toe, over and over, she rolled over my back and landed on her feet. I twirled her three times then took her hands and slid her between my legs, stepping over her head and bringing her back upright. She bopped backwards, and then did a cartwheel as I ducked and lifted her butt with my shoulder so she could slide down my back. We held hands above our heads as we twirled, her clockwise, me counter-clockwise. The band rocked with songs by Little Richard, Elvis Presley, Chuck Berry, Bo Diddley, and Bill

Haley and the Comets. The judges circulated around the dance floor, tapping various couples on their shoulders. We rocked 'till there were no other couples on the dance floor. We knew we had won. They let us keep on rockin' to the cheers of the crowd. Finally the music stopped, and we were declared the winners. The manager presented us with a giant "Pabst Blue Ribbon," and a check for 25 dollars, both of which I gave to Carrie. My little sister was so excited.

It was late when we left the Neptune Club, but we were hungry, so we stopped and ate some burgers at a Krystal on the way back home. It was the only place to eat that was still open.

It was 2:30 a.m. when we arrived at the house. As Sharon and I stood in the upstairs hallway kissing each other goodnight, Carrie and Squid each said their goodnights, entered their respective rooms, and closed their doors. I put my finger to my mouth and whispered, "shhh," as I reached over and closed Sharon's door, then led her quietly down the hall to my room. I did the right thing, because the love making was fabulous, as usual, quiet, but fabulous.

I woke Sharon early so she could sneak back down the hall to her room. I climbed in the shower, dressed, and then opened my door to head down the hall to the staircase. I only took a few steps when Carrie's door opened. Squid and Carrie departed from Carrie's room together. I mean, they left the confines of her room at the same time, and stepped out into the hall side-by-side. Squid had the biggest shit-eating grin that I have ever seen on his face in the two years that I have known him.

"No," I said. "You two didn't get it on last night. Did you? Not my sister and my roommate. No, say it isn't true." Actually, they both had shit-eating grins on their faces.

"April fool!" Squid said.

"April fool!" Carrie chimed in.

I thought for a minute, and then realized that tomorrow was April Fools Day. "Are you two putting me on? Did you, or did you not, make love to each other last night?"

"April fool!" said Squid again.

"April fool!" Carrie repeated, as their grins turned to laughter.

"Let's go down to the breakfast table and discuss this matter," I said.

"We are not going to discuss this matter, as you call it, at the breakfast table or anywhere else," said Carrie.

"I have spent months trying to get my roommate laid. And, I am always trying to protect my sister. And, the two of you walk out of Carrie's room with shit-eating grins on your faces and tell me 'April fool,' without any further explanation. What in the hell am I supposed to think?"

"If, and I am saying if, Carrie and I really made love, you should be happy that I am no longer a virgin, and that you had something to do with that accomplishment," said Squid.

"Not with my sister!" I said.

"If, and I am saying if, Squid and I really made love, you should be happy that you caught me with somebody that you know and care about, rather than somebody you didn't know," said Carrie.

"Not with my roommate!" I said, as they both burst out laughing again. They continued to laugh, as they hung on to each other and descended the stairs, heading toward the kitchen. Were they really putting me on? If so, they were doing a good job of it. April fool, my ass, I thought. All of a sudden they were acting awfully cozy together. I'll bet they did it. Yeah, I'll bet they really did it. Then I didn't know what to think. I mean, I have known all along that Carrie wasn't a virgin, so if they did it, big deal. And, I should be glad, after all my trouble to get Squid laid, that he is no longer a virgin, if in fact he is no longer a virgin, but with my sister. About that time, Sharon came into the kitchen and wanted to know what was so funny. Carrie and Squid just burst out laughing again.

Squid sat down at one end of the table, and Carrie sat down in his lap. She put her arms around him and gave him a big kiss. Well, I definitely hadn't seen them act like that before. They must have done it.

Squid laughed and said, "Actually, Deano, er Dean, I was just in Carrie's room helping her hang the 'Pabst Blue Ribbon' on her wall." They both started laughing again. Sharon was putting two and two together and started chuckling herself. They sure had me going.

Have you ever wanted to know the answer to something, and the longer you didn't know, the more you wanted to know? That was the case with me. Finally, I said, "Don't you think I deserve to know? If I promise not to hold it against either of you, will you answer my question, truthfully? Did you two make love last night?"

Carrie and Squid looked at each other, she was still sitting in his lap, they both smiled, and
in unison they chimed, "Yes!"

Sharon jumped up from her chair and hugged both of them together. "Congratulations!"
she said.

I was not so enthusiastic, but I still had to grin.

Dad walked into the kitchen, so we immediately changed the subject.

"Dad, I found the perfect car for Carrie. It is like new."
"Tell me about it," inquired Dad.

"It's a baby blue Henry J., made by Kaiser, and it only has 2,000 miles on it. It was driven by an old lady who never went anywhere."

"Why is it for sale?" Dad asked.

"She died!" I said.

Carrie asked, "Did she die in the car?"

CHAPTER FORTY-THREE

Snow on Calvary

Carrie planned to stay at Sharon's house Saturday night, so after spending the afternoon and evening with the girls, we dropped them off at Sharon's about midnight. We doubled back to Sharon's house Easter morning, picked them up again and went to breakfast before going to St. Theresa Catholic Church for late-morning mass.

Of course, being Easter, the church was full. Folding chairs were brought in from the parish hall and placed along the outer aisles to handle some of the overflow, but part of the congregation had to stand. Besides the four of us, Mom and Dad were present. I noticed that Linda and her parents were in attendance, as well as many other people that I knew. What a great time for a prank. It was unusual for Easter to fall on April Fool's Day. Squid and I knew we had to take advantage of it. I sure hoped that nobody would consider it sacrilegious, because that wasn't our intent. But, Squid and I had planned a really good one.

Standing high on the altar at St. Theresa Catholic Church is a crucifix, a statue of Christ on the cross. Behind, and above, the crucifix is a backdrop of tall organ pipes that extend about 20 feet above the top of the cross. There is no organist, however, for either the early-morning or mid-morning services. Hymns are sung to music piped through the high-fidelity speakers in the church. Late-morning mass is a different story. Wilbur Williams is a fine organist, and he plays with enthusiasm, getting the maximum sound possible out of those tall organ pipes. His arms and his head move with emphasis as he strokes the keys and depresses the pedals. The church is nearly always packed for late-morning mass, due in part to the marvelous playing of Wilbur Williams. As one faces the altar, the organ is on the right, and the choir on the left.

Knowing that the church would be empty between the early-morning and mid-morning services, Squid and I sneaked in and climbed up on the platform behind the organ pipes. We poured eight bags of Gold Bond bleached flour into the tops of the pipes, before we headed to Sharon's house to pick up the girls for breakfast. Our pancakes were good, and we headed to church.

Everyone was settled in their pews. The choir stood for the opening rite, and the congregation rose as well. The procession consisted of the crucifer (cross bearer), two altar boys, the deacon, a visiting priest, and the pastor of St. Theresa's parish. They were ready to start down the aisle as Wilbur Williams raised his hands to sound the first notes on the organ. It was time for all hell to break loose. As Mr. Williams' fingers struck the keyboard, the choir began, *Jesus Christ is risen today..."* At that instant white clouds came billowing out from the mouths and tops of the organ pipes. Wilbur Williams continued to play, and the choir sang on, as the procession strolled down the aisle. All the while it looked like a blizzard of snow was covering the altar. The congregation broke out in laughter, and the laughter turned to howls, as Mr. Williams played on.

"Holy shit, Squid, look at that snow storm," I said.

"You didn't have anything to do with that, did you?" asked Sharon as she laughed.

She knew me well. I said, "How could I have? I was with the three of you this morning."

THE CURTAIN FALLS

Where did they go from here?

LINDA and PEACHY:

Became nuns at St. Joseph's Monastery. After serving there for four years, they were both dismissed for having a lesbian affair with each other.

WANDA:

Shot her boyfriend, Jake, and was sentenced to twenty-five years imprisonment at the Florida State Penitentiary, in Raiford. She served only three of those years, however, before being released.

WILLIE:

Died two years after we graduated from Kane Military, when he choked to death on some of his own sauerkraut.

ELVIN McCALL:

Joined the Ku Klux Klan, but ceremoniously passed away during one of their rallies when a burning cross fell on his head.

TINA:

Became a multi-millionaire when the old man she married kicked the bucket. She used part of her inheritance to open a mail order bikini business.

BONES GIFFORD:

Became a swimming instructor at KMA. He drowned when he bumped his head during a life saving drill, and nobody jumped in the pool to save him.

BILLY:

Wilhelm von Kreisler III slept intimately with his aunt until she died at age 87. He was 63. She left him everything she had, including one million dollars worth of stocks and bonds, and her stainless steel 1981 DeLorean DMC-12 sports car.

RONALD BECKUM:

He was paranoid about water, so he forevermore wore a floatation device around his waist every time he climbed into a bath tub.

ZEBRA:

Dyed the white streaks in his hair black, and then changed his nickname to Bear.

CRAWFISH:

Returned to New Orleans. A few months after graduating from Tulane University, he was run over and crushed by a Mardi Gras float while diving for a nickels worth of plastic beads.

CAPTAIN BOHANON:

BoBo kept on teaching chemistry at KMA. He eventually covered all of the "I Like Ike" stickers on his old Hudson, with some new ones that read, "For Honesty and Integrity elect Richard Nixon."

RAY:

Put a mattress in the back of his Rambler, and spent the rest of his life sleeping in a different place every night.

ROONEY:

Got so carried away with his custom work that he painted bright orange flames leaping from the windows and doors of his house.

LEONARDO:

After his teenage daughter informed him that she wanted to become a stripper, he sold his bar. Soon thereafter he built a flophouse for the homeless.

SUGAR:

With an owner's share of 20%, she and four other strippers opened an after hours bottle club and strip joint called "Sugar and Spice."

COUNTY LINE GUY:

Died from an infection incurred when he was bitten by a Doberman pinscher.

WILBUR WILLIAMS:

Stopped playing the organ at St. Theresa's after he was caught in the confession booth giving the visiting pastor a blow job.

TRAIN MAN:

Somebody gave him a mine worker's helmet, equipped with a bright light, so he could run up and down the railroad tracks at night, which he did.

HOWARD HILL:

Got his wish to be buried in a boat. After being released from the reformatory, he attempted to reach the north shore of Cuba in order to join Fidel Castro's rebel army. A mortar shell shot by Fulgencio Batista's men sank Hill and his boat to the bottom of the Caribbean.

BRAD:

His marriage to Karen Marin lasted less than six months. She caught him screwing Miss Mary Ann in the building next door and filed for divorce. Brad moved back home and lived with his parents until he was age 47, at which time he took up residency with a female impersonator named Pat.

KAREN:

After kicking Brad out for one affair, she became a "momma" in her brother Tank's motorcycle gang. She banged the whole gang with regularity (except, possibly, her brother, Tank).

DAD, MOM & SUSAN:

Dad sold his controlling interest in the shipyard and bought a 110 foot Hatteras yacht. Dad and Mom spent the rest of their days touring the world. Susan went with them to do the cooking on board. The yacht even had a color television. Once again, Dad and Mom had separate bedrooms.

JUNIOR:

Finally gave up trying to build a fast hot rod, and went to work for the Tire Jungle selling retreads and used tires.

TANK:

He lost his tattooed right forearm one night in a wreck on his Harley. According to Karen, a drunk tree stepped out in front of him. He continued to ride thereafter using a hook on his throttle.

JOSEPH ABSALOM:

Became United States Ambassador to somewhere – possibly Antarctica.

ARTIE MANN:

Got a part-time job at the Starwood Stables and spent the next few years shoveling horse shit while he attended college and graduate school.

"SISTER" MARY LOUISE:

While in jail in Savannah, Georgia, she pickpocketed the keys to the exit doors and escaped, never to be heard from again.

NASTY NELLIE:

Became a United States census taker, so she could solicit her wares from door to door.

MISS MARY ANN:

After she was eventually terminated at Kane Military for illicit behavior, Miss Mary Ann moved to Washington, D.C. She made national news when she was caught having affairs with two married U.S. Senators. Her new found fame launched Miss Boobs into the centerfold of Playboy magazine.

MAJOR HARDEN:

Hard-ass became so obsessed with protecting the integrity of Kane Military Academy that it drove him insane. Bess Harden had him committed to the state psychiatric center at Chattahoochee.

TEDDY McCORMICK:
Was decapitated when he drove his Chevy convertible under a tractor that was towing a hay wagon.

BERTHA:
Was hired by Leonardo to help staff the flophouse. He was certain that she was so ugly, that none of the sex addicts, drug addicts or psychologically disturbed tenants would mess with her.

SHARON & DEAN:
Sharon became Miss Florida, but had her crown stripped when she married Dean, halfway through her reign. When the 1957 Chevys hit the streets, Dean no longer had the fastest car in town so he decided that it was time to slow down. Sharon received her BA in Political Science at the University of Florida, while Dean graduated with a degree in Engineering. Dean and Sharon moved into the house on the Ortega River where they lived happily ever after. Carrie's old bedroom remained unchanged: Pabst Blue Ribbon, fancy pink phone with the sparkling dial, and all. She used to comment during occasional visits that it seemed so weird to return to the house she grew up in, and to see her best friend living there. Sharon and Dean obviously never figured out what caused kids. They had to hire a nanny, cook and house-keeper to help them take care of their eleven kids.

SQUID & CARRIE:
Squid enrolled at Harvard University, but flunked out at the end of his freshman year. His philosophy of reading *Dick Tracy* comic books instead of studying didn't work very well at Harvard. He returned to Jacksonville, married Carrie, and they moved to Miami. Squid took over the charter fleet after his father died (probably from over-badgering). The *Lady Mae* was renamed the *Lady Carrie*, much to the chagrin of Squid's mother who still did not have a boat named after her. Carrie remained the only female ever laid by Squid for the entirety of his life.

Acknowledgements

The author's sincere appreciation goes out to the following people:

Richard Southworth
Harold Flanders
Russell Higginbotham
Mary Monroe
Bill Phillips
Faye Franklin
Chip Southworth
Michele Snethkamp
Steve Campbell
Herb Gable
David Valenzuela
Joy Rissmiller
Madeline Meehan
Judy Von Koenig

9 781890 778118

BULL
IN THE
RING

A NOVEL